Giovanni Rests In Pieces

The Med School Series, Volume 6

Kathy Bryson

Published by Kathy Bryson, 2021.

GIOVANNI RESTS IN PIECES

First edition. July 3, 2021.

Copyright © 2021 Kathy Bryson.

ISBN: 979-8201727543

Written by Kathy Bryson.

Table of Contents

To Karen J, who came up with the perfect title!

And with many thanks to everyone who helped Giovanni throughout his journey!

Chapter 1

"I don't know what you expect her to do!" The woman standing in front of Giovanni had gotten steadily shriller as she protested, so now her voice was approaching auditory levels only dogs could hear. Giovanni smiled tightly but didn't try to respond because all of his efforts so far had only gotten him more piercing accusations.

"Do you know how long it's taken us just to get this far? Do you know how many people don't answer their phones or don't call back how, how many secretaries we've gone through who just don't care if someone's dying and can't even be bothered to take a message?!" The woman paused for breath, gasping to a temporary halt.

Giovanni noticed the attending nurse roll her eyes behind the shrieking woman and winced, not wanting to get caught in the endless battle between frantic patient and overworked nurse. His patient, an older woman with brown hair going white, tried ineffectively to stop her companion.

"Rita, that's enough." She reached out a hand that had a peripheral line taped to it. It shook slightly, but her other hand rested in her lap, seemingly calmer. Giovanni suspected she was simply too weak to move it without effort.

"I know it's frustrating, Ma'am," he started, wanting to help his patient and wanting to be anywhere else at the same time, "but–"

"They're doing the best they can," the older lady continued as if she hadn't heard him. She lightly patted him on the arm, her fingertips a mere brush of skeletal digits.

Her sister was not pacified. She actually stomped her foot. "No, Margie, he is going to give us some answers if I have to stand right here all day!"

Giovanni could feel himself growing angry. His head hurt and his jaw ached from where he gritted his teeth. Some of his irritation was just fatigue. Despite having fewer classes, entering clinical rotations in his third year of medical school was exhausting. Even the practice he'd gotten working as a medical clerk or volunteering at the free clinic hadn't prepared him for the onslaught of demands. Everybody had a question or a comment or wanted something right away. He still worked nights in the morgue sometimes, not because he had to, but because he couldn't sleep if he went home. His ears just rang from all the noise of the day. The morgue at least was quiet.

The fact that Rita probably had legitimate complaints was equally irritating. Giovanni was tempted to protest himself. Even as a student, Giovanni had to tackle obtaining medical records from outside institutions, following up on tests, and writing up treatment recommendations. And he wasn't even technically administration or a doctor! But sympathetic as he was to the lady's complaints about the American medical system, he really couldn't do much to reform it right now, and Rita was preventing him from doing what he could.

"Ma'am, I appreciate your concern, but right now what I need is to examine your sister and you're blocking access to my patient."

Pulling his tablet up closer to his chest, Giovanni glared at the middle-aged woman who sputtered, but stepped aside. Giovanni kept the frown going, but inwardly he was relieved. It wasn't like him to come off as tough; in fact, he was surprised he'd been able to pull it off. Deliberately not looking at the nurse who was smirking suspiciously, he forced a smile and pulled the privacy curtain closed. "Hello, ma'am. I just need ask you a few questions."

Margie wasn't nearly as difficult as her sister, but Giovanni could tell she was nervous. Since he didn't have to do more than get her vitals before handing her off to his supervising physician, he left the curtain open enough that she could see her sister.

"Your name is Marguerite Suarez?" he asked, peering at his chart. "Margie for short? Wait, is your sister also Marguerite? Rita for short?"

Margie nodded, the corners of her eye crinkling to almost shut as she smiled. "Oh yes, my mother couldn't make up her mind, so my father just picked a name he could remember. My mother was also Marguerite."

The irate lady outside the curtain rolled her eyes, but his patient laughed, pleased he'd caught what was apparently a family joke.

"That's crazy," Giovanni laughed, relieved to be on better footing with his patient. "I'm named after a great uncle myself. Can you stretch out your arm? This might pinch a little, but just long enough to get your blood pressure. Oh, thank you." This last was to the nurse who silently handed him a fingertip oximeter.

"Your names must have made life easier for your dad," Giovanni said to Margie.

This time, Rita laughed outside the curtain. "Not really," she said. "We just pretended we didn't know who he was calling."

Giovanni grinned. "Way to work your dad."

"Are you having any gastrointestinal distress with the feeding tube?" he turned back to Margie. "Upset stomach, diarrhea?"

"She farts like a trucker!" A young voice called from the hall.

"Hush you!" Rita scolded while Margie blushed. "My nephew," she whispered.

Giovanni couldn't stop the grin that spread across his face, so he made a show of checking his tablet. "I'll put down some discomfort."

"Um," Margie leaned forward, struggling to lift herself. Giovanni reached out and took her by the elbow to help. "Do you think I'll need this much longer? I mean, the feeding tube?"

Giovanni was uncomfortably aware of sudden attentive silence from outside the privacy curtain. "It's hard to say," he attempted to explain. "It's gonna depend on how well you continue healing and how your body responds."

Margie gave him a small, sad smile. "Yes, I suppose. Hopefully, I'll be fine, right?"

Giovanni looked pointedly at her sister peering around the privacy curtain. "You got a good support system," he told Margie. "You won't be fine, you are fine!"

Margie laughed, even as Rita jumped and stepped back for his supervising physician to pull the privacy curtain aside. Giovanni thought again that they need some way to rap on a door jamb except that multi-patient examining rooms didn't exactly have door jambs.

Dr. Patel held out his hand to Margie. "And how are you feeling today, my dear?" He took the tablet from Giovanni as she murmured, "fine, fine," glancing at it quickly.

"Fine? Are you sure, Margie?" Dr. Patel smiled warmly, setting the tablet down and pulling up a stool. "Gio says you're feeling some discomfort."

"Um, digestive distress," Giovanni murmured.

"She farts!" came the voice from hall.

Dr. Patel tried not grin but failed. Coughing, he looked back down at the tablet. "Any pain then?"

"Well, no, not really." Margie's attention seemed equally divided between the doctor and the hall. Outside the privacy curtain, Giovanni could see Rita starting to open her mouth.

"Shall we take a look then?" Dr. Patel interjected smoothly. "Gio will go get your family's medical history," and Giovanni found himself outside the curtain holding the tablet.

Giovanni wasn't sure what medical history he was supposed to get, but he understood he was being dismissed. It wasn't the most comfortable feeling coming from his supervising physician, but he was pretty sure it wasn't personal. Every doctor had their own way of dealing with patients, and apparently Dr. Patel's was to use his students as a block. Still, if Dr. Patel wasn't as nurturing as Dr. Beverly from his psych rotation, he was still good about sharing information and letting Giovanni take the lead on rounds. And being sent out into the hall wasn't the worst interaction he'd ever had with a supervising physician. Once he'd actually dropped a snake on one, sending that particular attending physician to his own emergency room.

Right now, however, he had to deal with Rita. She stood with arms crossed, staring him down.

"You've got our family history," she said. "I've told the nurses, the doctors, everyone who asked over and over everything I can remember about vaccinations, illnesses, my mother, my father, everything I can remember. Read your machine there!"

Giovanni glanced down at his tablet automatically, but Rita wasn't finished.

"And since you already have that info, now maybe you can tell me just what you're doing here."

Giovanni opened his mouth and hesitated while Rita carried on.

"You recommended surgery, you recommended chemo, all this treatment that just ended up with her in rehab. Now you're telling us feeding tube. How long? What are the consequences?"

Giovanni gaped like a floundering fish under the onslaught of the sister's questions, not so much because he didn't have the answers, but because he wasn't sure how much he could share. Somebody somewhere had to have told the family something, following protocol if nothing else, but he hadn't been part of those conversations, and he didn't want to contradict what Rita had already been told.

She was mad enough already. Giovanni lifted his tablet, an unconscious wave of surrender, but Rita ground on relentless.

"How is that good care? Just what is it you're doing here? We haven't gotten any information, and now we're back again with more complications, more bills, more things to TRY, and still no answers!"

Even knowing and understanding the woman's frustration, Giovanni felt himself tense. His shoulders hunched and his head lowered even as he told himself that he didn't have to answer, he didn't have to justify himself. It was just an autonomic response to attack, but that thought didn't help as he scrambled for an answer.

'Hello, hello!" a cherry voice rang out.

Startled, Giovanni looked up to see his former boss hurrying down the corridor towards him. Mr. Lively had been the morgue manager until a too-close encounter with vampire-controlled rats had forced him into the psych ward and early retirement. The morgue management had been taken over by the residents supervising students with mixed results. Giovanni had been both relieved of and taken on more responsibilities, but he couldn't complain since the rats had been his fault – sort-of.

Mr. Lively came up to their small group and held out his hand, beaming. "I heard there was some confusion over your coverage," he began.

"Uh, Mr. Lively, Rita…" and Giovanni looked down at his tablet, embarrassed to realize he'd been addressing a grown woman by her given name. His nonnas would have thumped him good. "Uh, Suarez. Mrs. Suarez, Mr. Lively."

"Hernandez," Rita corrected him. "We only have the same first name."

Mrs. Hernandez shook Mr. Lively's hand perfunctorily, her attention and ire still directed at Giovanni.

Mr. Lively surprised her, however. "I'm here to help you navigate your insurance claim," he said.

Giovanni blinked. He knew Mr. Lively had been reassigned since he was technically not old or insane enough for actual retirement, but he hadn't realized Mr. Lively had become a patient advocate. Mrs. Hernandez turned eagerly to him, mouth opening for another impassioned defense of her sister.

"Yes, yes, I agree, the insurance is ridiculous. So many rules," Mr. Lively responded before being asked. "The thing is to ignore all of them and just persevere. It's like pushing through a bush. Just keep going and don't stop to look at the leaves."

Mrs. Hernandez blinked at him, mouth agape.

Mr. Lively smiled at her, serene and happy. "Now which of these names do you recognize?" and he spread a sheaf of forms wide like a hand of playing cards.

Giovanni stepped quietly back as Mrs. Hernandez and Mr. Lively began plowing through the stack of paperwork. He wasn't entirely surprised at the man's efficiency. Mr. Lively had been a good manager, just too nervous for the odd going-ons in the morgue. And Giovanni certainly wasn't going to interfere with anyone who could actually navigate the morass of paperwork the hospital generated!

Dr. Patel must have had the same idea because he waved urgently at Giovanni to follow as he slipped out of the examining room and headed down the hall. He only slowed long enough to take the tablet from Giovanni and leave it at the nurse's station. Pushing the button for the elevator, Dr. Patel spoke quietly, keeping his gaze fixed ahead. "Best to let the admin handle Mrs. Hernandez. It's nice that she's looking after her sister, but she does get worked up."

Giovanni hesitated, then blurted out. "Someone had discussed Mrs. Suarez's prognosis with the family, right?"

Dr. Patel sighed. "Of course. But how blunt do you want to be?"

He turned his head slightly to look in Giovanni's direction. "You handled that well when you told her she had a good support system. She does. It may make all the difference. Does it help to tell her that the statistics are against her?"

He sighed and faced the closed elevator door again. "I don't know whether it's better or not to tell her it's 50-50 whether she gets off the feeding tube, that she may not last more than a year, but right now, she has hope. She's happy. She has the right to know, but if I tell her, then maybe she spends the year waiting in despair, anxious, or maybe not. You can't tell the patient their options if you say it in a way that's going to make their situation worse."

He sighed and poked the elevator button again. "What is with this elevator? You'd think someone was trapped in it."

Chapter 2

Rounds over, Giovanni headed down to the hospital basement to start his second job as the morgue night shift. He had seriously considered giving up that job when he started rotations, but he had grown to like the quiet there. Between his three roommates, sometimes the house he shared felt a lot like Grand Central Station even if he did spend less and less time there.

He didn't have to work late fortunately as he was already tired but after two and a half years of looking after the morgue, Giovanni couldn't go home without checking in. Especially after Mr. Lively left and the day shift was taken over by a rotating cast of first year medical students. They weren't unsupervised of course, but it wasn't the same as when Mr. Lively was in charge.

Upon reflection, Giovanni wasn't surprised that Mr. Lively was on top of insurance. He had kept brilliant records for the morgue. It was only the rats that got to him. Well, that and the cockroaches and ghosts and vampires and werewolves.

Giovanni sighed. Most of that was not his fault, he knew that, but he still couldn't help but feel some guilt over what had happened to Mr. Lively. The nervous little man had not deserved to be attacked by rats. Still, he seemed happy enough to handling patients. Just goes to show, you never knew what someone was capable of.

The muffled sound of a radio greeted him as he stepped off the elevator. Per the guidelines he'd helped draw up, any music had to be kept low and tuned to an easy listening station. Families and friends, coming to collect their loved ones, shouldn't be subjected to pounding beats or obnoxious lyrics.

The office was empty, however. Giovanni frowned at the scattered piles of books and papers even as he looked around for the student who was supposed to be on duty. Whoever it was, they better not have left the morgue unattended and especially not in such a mess. He dumped his backpack on top of a desk and headed to the counter and coffeepot against the far wall. When a harried looking young woman came hurrying in, Giovanni was standing glaring at the open door, one eyebrow pulled down into a fierce scowl.

"Sorry," the woman panted. "I had to go pee, and no one's been by, so..."

Giovanni hastily smoothed out his expression even as the girl's voice trailed off and she peered askance at him.

"Are you alright?" she asked. "You look a little, uh...?"

"I'm fine," Giovanni answered hastily. "Fine, everything's fine."

"Good," the girl said. "Because I was thinking nauseated, bilious, dyspeptic, constipated. That coffee will kill you."

Somewhere between embarrassed and baffled, Giovanni peered down at his cup. Maybe he should have made a fresh pot.

"Anyway, I'm glad you're here," the girl went on. "I really need to take off early to get to the library. Only one patient came in," and she tugged a file folder out from underneath the teetering pile, "so it's not like you'll be busy."

Giovanni took the file folder automatically and opened his mouth to protest, then shut it firmly. No, he wasn't going to yell after the woman fleeing down the hall towards the elevators. He had a better idea. Giovanni hadn't acted irresponsibly when he'd been a freshman medical student and first started working at the morgue. Fred, the orderly, who'd delivered his first patient, wouldn't have put up with it. And remembering how Fred had dealt with other morgue issues, Giovanni knew exactly how to handle the mess he'd walked into.

An hour later, the desks were cleared, the floor swept, and the countertops wiped clean. Giovanni couldn't bring himself to throw away expensive textbooks, so those were piled neatly on one counter, but everything else that had been left lying, from notes to food wrappers, was now in large garbage bags at the loading dock waiting to be picked up with the rest of the hospital's trash. Giovanni was torn about whether or not to throw away wallets or purses, knowing what a hassle getting a license at GDOT could be, so he'd locked those away in a desk drawer and added the key to his own ring.

Sipping at his cup of freshly made coffee, Giovanni sat down to study the pile of morgue-related paperwork he'd pulled out as he cleared the mess away. Any guilt he might have felt quickly evaporated in light of the incomplete routing orders. No body should ever be released without signed authorization and receipt, but here were partial copies, the top half missing and only a bleary carbon left as well as some with a hasty scrawl that couldn't be deciphered into any meaningful name or directions. Doctors' handwriting had nothing on these sad scraps.

Giovanni picked up a slip of paper and was relieved to see that it wasn't an intake form, but a supply requisition. The hospital, like any large organization, ran on paper, but he was having trouble keeping up. The other papers were the routing forms for patients that, unfortunately, he couldn't locate in the morgue. Most likely, those people's remains had been claimed by relatives or funeral homes, but he couldn't find the final form with the receiving signature.

Giovanni sighed and laid the requisition down on an office desk. He didn't know where it got filed. They really needed the morgue manager back in charge, but Mr. Lively, after bouncing in and out of psychiatric treatment for hallucinations of paranormal phenomena, seemed to have happily landed in insurance claims adjustment. And Giovanni wasn't about to tell him that the rats and cockroaches that invaded were really a vampire plague. The poor guy was nervous enough as it was. But he had kept the paperwork under control.

He'd just finished sorting the scraps into some sort of order when he heard the elevator chime. Looking up, he saw a resident he knew and a student he didn't know.

"I thought we went over procedures," Giovanni addressed the resident. "Why are there still unsigned receipts here? No one comes or goes without a signature!"

Huntington sat down with a sigh and took the bundle of papers Giovanni waved at him. A big man with blond hair, he looked cramped behind a desk, but seemed indifferent to any discomfort as he scanned the papers. "Again? I swear to God, we have gone over this and over this!"

The student was young and thin in a generic sort of way that would have made him hard to pick out of a full classroom. His uniform of brand name t-shirt and jeans did nothing to help distinguish him. "Um, where are my notes?" he asked, blinking as he looked around.

"If you mean the trash that was left on these desks, then with the rest of the garbage near the loading docks," Giovanni replied, not looking up from his papers.

'The student yelped and took off running.

Huntington twisted in his chair to watch him go, then turned back to Giovanni. "You threw away his notes?"

"I threw away everything," Giovanni declared flatly. He was still pissed and didn't bother to soften his tone. "This is not a frat house. They need to show some respect and keep it clean."

"Cool." Huntington grinned, then hastily straightened his face into a more sober expression as Giovanni glared. "Hey, you'll get no arguments from me. I told them. I even growled."

Giovanni, who'd never been able to maintain anger for very long anyway, let it go and turned back to his papers. "They're idiots. Were we ever that dumb?"

"Yes," a deep voice growled from the hall.

Giovanni smiled to himself at the gruff insult. Fred was an elderly orderly who may have seemed harsh and unforgiving but who'd also bailed him out of more than one bad scrape. Fred was also the head of a mysterious secret society that attempted to contain the odd occurrences around the hospital including both Giovanni's ghost and werewolf, which really wasn't that surprising actually. Everyone knew secretaries and janitors really ran the world.

"Sir." Giovanni started to stand, then he jumped startled as he saw who accompanied Fred. "Matias, what are you doing here? God, not another pile-up?!" And he pressed one hand to his heart, remembering the aftermath of the last car collision he'd had to process through the morgue.

"Nah, nah, nothing bad," Matias assured him, waving one hand in dismissal. "I'm interviewing for your job."

Giovanni drew back, seriously alarmed for a moment. He worked so hard to get through medical school that any hiccup in this last semester would probably end him. Then he smiled in relief as realization dawned. "You're the new morgue manager? Oh my God, that would be so great!"

Huntington jumped to his feet and reached for Matias's hand. "So great," he echoed, pumping furiously. "We really need help down here."

"Told you," Fred rumbled, a wry twist quirking one corner of his mouth. "They mean well, but these baby docs couldn't organize their way out of the open end of a paper bag."

"I'm a pediatrician," Huntington told him. "Gio's a GP." And Fred shook his head.

Matias frowned and looked around, gently extricating his hand from Huntington's clasp as he did so. "I don't know. It looks pretty clean."

"That's because Giovanni threw everything away," Huntington said.

"Everything?!" Matias frowned, alarmed.

"Yes, everything! Including my notes!" The thin student was back, hauling a bulging trash bag with him.

"Get that out of here!" Fred roared. "Don't you know the morgue has to be kept clean?"

The student blinked and scrambled back into the hall, still carrying his garbage sack. "Where am I supposed to dump this then?" he asked.

"In the garbage!" Giovanni and Huntington yelled together.

The thin student blinked and headed back down the hall to the loading deck, mumbling something Giovanni chose to ignore. Fred watched him go, one eyebrow lowered threateningly, then turned back to the morgue office.

"You two show Matias around," he started, then the lights flickered and went out.

In the dark, Giovanni heard a deep, heavy sigh, then Fred's voice rumbled, "Fine, you tell Matias the basic procedures while I call maintenance."

"The morgue is where we hold any "celestial discharges.' Those are patients who pass until someone comes to claim the body. Usually a funeral home, sometimes a family member," Huntington started.

"Suspicious deaths might pass through on their way to the Medical Examiner's office, but we don't do autopsies here. Those are done in the labs upstairs if there's anything the doctors need to verify about cause of death. Mostly we're here to keep everything quiet," Giovanni explained. "Don't want to upset any patients or families upstairs. We want them to think whatever treatment they're getting will work." He swallowed hard, pushing way the memory of Ms. Suarez.

Matias nodded. "Sounds pretty straightforward. Check them in and check them out. So, what's the problem then?" And he nodded towards the paperwork. "Someone not claimed?"

"No, anyone without family goes to the funeral home anyway," Fred told him. "We've got a partnership with several around town to process unclaimed bodies. There's procedures."

"That's the problem," Giovanni confided to his roommate. "The process should be completely transparent. We should know where everyone is and where they went at all times. Whoever's been checking these bodies out isn't leaving a complete paper trail."

"I think I've got this." Huntington peered at a paper using his cellphone for light. "I think this says Bonnie Anne. Is that one of our partner mortuaries?"

Giovanni almost rolled his eyes but held back even as he realized no one could see him. Even so, he couldn't keep from speaking abruptly to the burly resident. "No that's not one of ours. Did you check the log? It's not just the signature on the outtake form. They're also supposed to be entered on the log."

Giovanni could hear the large man shuffling around even if he couldn't see him in the dim lighting of the emergency lights. He could see Matias, however, who appeared to be grinning.

"The computer won't boot up," Huntington announced in the darkness, and this time Giovanni did roll his eyes.

"I'll have to check the log later," the resident went on. "It says 'medical science research services' in the type of business column. Is that the same as mortuary?"

Giovanni frowned. The column for type of business usually had only two responses, funeral home or family. Sometimes someone got fancy and put in "cremation services" or some such, but "medical research" was a new one. He quirked an eyebrow at Fred, then felt an idiot for trying to communicate by expression in the dark.

"Shouldn't be any medical research through the morgue," Fred rumbled anyway. "Any organ donations would start with the doctor and go through Patient Services and whatever other departments apply. Could be half a dozen easily. Whole other process there with the feds – Division of Transplantation with Health and Human Services for starters."

"Okay, well that's not it, obviously," Huntington mused. He peered more closely at the paper, his nose a stark silhouette against his phone's light. "Maybe it's like last time when we thought the body got put in backup storage but probably got put in the sub-basement."

"This is a regular thing? Bodies going missing?" Matias asked. He lowered his voice, but Giovanni was pretty sure Fred still heard every word. "You didn't say anything about bodies going missing."

"No!" Giovanni protested. "Everyone's been accounted for. It's just not clear who they were passed off to. The paperwork's the problem, not the backup unit. We don't even use the backup unit."

"Well, there's only one other place to look." Huntington straightened up and laid his phone down even as the elevator chimed and two men stepped out, powerful flashlight beams bouncing ahead of them.

Chapter 3

Tom and Jerry probably made record time getting to the basement, but the wait seemed interminable to Giovanni. He liked Fred, but the old man was intimidating, and Huntington pretty much destroyed any joking mood when he kept discussing all the paperwork confusion in the office. The tall, skinny student sulked at one end of the hall as he picked through the trash, Huntington hummed softly to himself as he sorted through the paperwork Giovanni had collected, and Fred glowered at all of them from underneath heavy, frowning brows. Giovanni didn't think Fred was actually mad, but he was relieved when the janitors spoke up and he had something else to focus on.

"What the hell are you doing to the lights?" one figure boomed.

The other figure appeared to bob behind the first, his shadow a vague shadow against the prevailing gloom, but Giovanni knew both men.

"Hi Tom, Hi Jerry," he greeted them.

"Get on the breakers for this floor right away," Fred boomed. "Are lights out on all levels?"

The three men huddled in the hall, stepping over and ignoring the medical student who squeaked and hastily grabbed at the trash bags spread around him, moaning louder when his phone fell inside one.

"I think we have to go into the sub-basement," Huntington said. He peered more closely at the papers he'd spread out over a desk. "I'm pretty sure SB means sub-basement."

Giovanni took the sheaf of papers away from Huntington and smoothed them out on his desktop. He'd only heard about the sub-basement last semester. He hadn't been so much astonished as baffled. After all, he had worked on the hospital lower levels for nearly three years, yet he'd had no idea there were more levels underneath the morgue. "We're not going into the sub-basement. We were told specifically to stay out of there."

"But what does SB mean if not sub-basement? We already checked the backup storage unit. And besides that's BS, not SB." Huntington threw up his hands.

Giovanni frowned at his colleague, but he was pretty sure the tall man facing him didn't mean what he'd actually said. Oversized and burly, Huntington still came off as the picture of innocence with his curly blond locks and wide-open, baby blue eyes.

"I don't think there's anything down there that we use," Giovanni said. "It's certainly not where we store any patient overflow."

"Well, there's nothing in the morgue and nothing in the backup unit," Huntington replied. "Certainly not any of these people." He peered again at the papers.

"You've lost another one? Seriously dude, why do they let you in here?" The two janitors stepped back into the office morgue, flashlights bobbing in front of them. One of the janitors looked laughingly at his partner.

The other man just rolled his eyes and stepped over to examine the breaker box. "Stay out of the sub-basement!" he barked.

"We already tried that, and I didn't lose another one," Giovanni protested. "There's just some glitches in the paperwork. Paperwork other students did, I might add!"

The student at the end of the hall huffed a little and turned his back to the group of men in the morgue office.

Huntington hesitated. "Um, maybe we should check it anyway. I mean these bodies probably just didn't get signed out properly, but we have to have a record. You can't just lose an unclaimed body."

"These are all unclaimed bodies?" Matias asked. He peered interestedly at the sheaf of papers Huntington pawed through, but Fred frowned even more fiercely than before.

Matias poked through the other papers. "We need to check this out," he said. "Georgia law is very clear. Twenty-four hours to claim a body, then they have to be preserved for sixty days before being released to a college or other educational institution. And they all have to be reported to the Board for the Distribution of Cadavers. Travelers dying unexpectedly have to be held for seventy-two hours. Suspicious deaths go to the Medical Examiner's Office. They don't even come here, but no one can just go missing."

Fred nodded, seemingly impressed. "S'good that you looked that up. Something our current employees should do maybe." And he bent his fierce gaze on Giovanni.

"Hey," Giovanni protested. "I never lost a body. She just sat up, then walked away. And I did sign her out. Her nephew took her!" His shoulders slumped as he remembered the incident that kicked off his medical career. He'd been frantic both to care for Mrs. Harris and to keep anyone from finding out she was a zombie. "I didn't lose her until after he brought her back, and then only because I was trying to fight vampires!" Somehow, having an excuse for driving Mrs. Harris away didn't make Giovanni feel any better.

A heavy hand clasped his shoulder for a minute, then Fred picked up one of the illegible forms and frowned at it. "Maybe we should check this out," he suggested. "Matias needs to see the whole set-up anyway if he's going to work here."

"Did you not just hear what Jerry just said?" Tom exclaimed. "We're not supposed to be down there!"

Fred leveled his daunting gaze at the janitor who gulped.

"We were told that area's off limits," Jerry interjected. He turned away from the breaker box with a sigh. "But I can't find a short here, so let's check out the mains. If you go somewhere while we're busy, we didn't see it. We'll try not to keep you in the dark."

Fred nodded once brusquely and gestured for Matias to follow him. Giovanni glanced towards Huntington and both men got up as well.

"The sub-basement is for emergencies," Fred told Matias.

"Um," Huntington started. "Isn't the emergency room upstairs?"

"Not that kind of emergency," Fred snapped. "National emergencies. The sub-basement is where we stockpile stuff in case of hurricanes or tornadoes. You know, real emergencies."

"Is this the only access?" Matias asked as they crowded into the emergency stairwell. Some doctors made a point of taking the stairs, but after slogging through miles of rounds, Giovanni had come to rely on the elevators.

"Nah, this is a sort of a back door. When you need to haul stuff in and out, the easiest way is through the freight elevator, back there near the loading dock," and Fred waved in that general direction.

"Can anyone access the freight elevator?" Matias asked. His voice was just a tad too mild, and Fred peered at him suspiciously.

"Yeah, sure, but why would they?"

"No reason," Matias shrugged one shoulder. "I'm an EMT. You see enough gunshot wounds, you start to think everyone's packing. Just my suspicious nature."

Giovanni mentally shrugged. He rode the central elevators near the hospital hub up and down all day long. Most people would have no reason to head to the back freight elevators unless they were hauling supplies or sometimes the occasional delivery to the morgue. There was a reason those elevators were out of sight.

Fred grunted and pushed on the fire door at the next landing. It opened into a large room, not a corridor, and for a moment, Giovanni blinked in the sudden light. Why the lights worked here and not one floor up was a mystery Tom and Jerry would have to solve.

The room wasn't the size of the ground floor of the hospital, but it was still extensive and filled with shelves overflowing with boxes. Most were unopened, but all were marked with assorted stickers from red biohazard labels to yellow chemical alerts. There was a lot of potentially dangerous material stored away down here. Giovanni was relieved to see lockers of hazmat gear and fire extinguishers along one wall. Ubiquitous clipboards hung from every shelf, most with pens still attached.

Fred led the small procession to the back end of the room, picking up and glancing at the occasional clipboard along the way, but not finding anything out of the ordinary apparently. He stopped before a long counter across the back and waved one hand towards it. "Well, that's the gist of it. You see anything that looks like a body?"

Giovanni circle around, scanning the few tables between racks of shelves and had to shake his head. He didn't see any refrigeration units or even the oversized drawer fronts found in the morgue that the unknowing might mistake for file cabinets. In fact, the place was surprisingly clean for storage with only a few odd items left out on the back counter...

"Hey, that's my espresso machine!" Delighted, Giovanni darted over and picked up the box. It was still sealed and only a little dusty.

"You remember," he told Fred, hugging the box. "It got thrown away by accident that semester you did the big inventory."

"I remember." Fred's voice was a wry as his expression. "That's the semester you tried living in the morgue." He shook his head, the action indicating as clearly as his tone of voice what he'd thought of that idea.

"Yeah, then you came to live with us." Matias peered around Fred's bulk at the box. "Are you sure that's it?" He sounded almost as excited as Giovanni.

"Yep," Giovanni nodded. "Look, it's still got the gift tag on it."

"Cool!" Huntington approved. "Funny that it ended up here. Is any of the rest of this yours?" And he waved at the assortment of glassware huddled around a small sink.

Giovanni glanced at two coffee carafes with obviously burnt bottoms, a small ceramic casserole dish with a hairline crack, and a tall, skinny glass vase filled with murky water and topped with a round-knobbed lid.

"Nope," he laughed. "This is all mine. I'm good."

Fred frowned again at the litter on the countertop, then seemed to push it away mentally. Clapping his hands together, he spun away and headed back to the stairwell. "All right, no bodies here. Let's close it up."

Headed back upstairs, Huntington stilled shuffled through papers, trying to make out signatures, but Giovanni, happy to have found his long-lost espresso machine, decided he'd done enough for one day.

"Check with the other students," he told the resident. "One of them has to remember having signed those bodies out."

Huntington frowned and for the first time, Giovanni heard a distinct edge to his voice. "One of them better remember. I'm not having my reputation ruined because someone couldn't follow directions."

Giovanni blinked, then shrugged off the comment. Huntington may have growled on occasion, but the big bear didn't usually get riled. Still, as the resident overseeing students in the morgue, he would look bad if someone really screwed up. After all the effort Giovanni had made to impress faculty and doctors at the hospital, he could sympathize. Those references weren't lightly earned.

"Well, let me know what you find out," he said. "I'll help as best I can."

The lights fared suddenly and both men looked up to see Tom hop lightly down from Jerry's shoulders. He gathered up the tools laying on the floor as Jerry shook out his arms and said, "Okay, that should do it. Try not to overload the breakers with another coffee machine, okay?"

"We didn't plug a new one in," Giovanni protested. "This was just stored downstairs."

"Yeah, yeah" Jerry said, scurrying after his fellow. "And stay out of the basement!"

Huntington watched them go, then turn to Giovanni. "That's going to be hard to do," he commented mildly, "since we are already in the basement."

"Wait for me," Giovanni called, and juggling the large box and his backpack awkwardly, ran to join the men headed upstairs.

He reached the elevator to the lobby just as the door started to close, so he tossed his backpack to Matias and slipped inside. Just as the elevator jerked to start its ascent, he heard a loud screech and felt himself hauled against the closed door panels. The waistband of his scrubs tightened alarmingly even as Giovanni found himself flipped upside down, his head now dangling under his feet that were reaching up towards the elevator car ceiling. Panicked, he clutched his espresso machine, so he didn't reach out to grab his scrubs caught in the elevator door as they peeled off his legs or to break his fall as he tumbled out of them onto his head.

Chapter 4

Giovanni scrambled to his feet, but the damage was already done. Still clutching his espresso machine, he pushed back his hair and winced at the gaping faces regarding him through the open door of the elevator. Behind him, he could hear a muffled snort even as the eyes of the gathered nurses drop slowly from his face to his feet, and their expressions change from horrified concern to hastily suppressed amusement. Mouths twisted and eyes flew in every direction as most of his colleagues tried not to laugh, but Dr. Perez felt no such hesitation.

"Jesus, Gio! Can't you keep your pants on for five minutes?"

The assembled company lost its collective composure as Dr. Perez reached out one arm to block the elevator door from closing. Reaching up, he snatched the scrap of fabric caught in the ceiling joints and held it out. "What is it with you and showing off your tidy-whities?"

Giovanni felt the air conditioning cool over his bare legs, but his face was hot and probably bright red. He held his head up, nose in the air, as he exited the elevator, but didn't acknowledge Dr. Perez. Matias was the one who took the shredded scrubs from the senior physician, his head ducked to hide a smile. Jerry was laughing so hard he had to lean against the wall of the elevator for support.

Fortunately, it was a short trip through the emergency room, but once outside, Giovanni wished he hadn't stalked off without his pants. Early spring temperatures in Atlanta were not that warm and a brisk breeze added to the chill. He hurried to his car and climbed in even as he heard Matias calling.

"Dude, don't drive off! I need a ride." Matias clambered into the passenger seat and held his hands out in front of the dashboard air vent.

Giovanni directed his best stink eye at his roommate.

"I'm sorry," Matias exclaimed even as he grinned. "It was funny!"

"I don't need you making fun of me where I work," Giovanni yelled. "They're never going to let me practice here even if I do pass the final boards."

"Yes, they will. Everyone needs a laugh," Matias blurted out, then held up both hands in protest. "Joking, joking!"

"I should make you walk home," Giovanni retorted and put the small sedan in gear. "How'd you get here anyway?"

"Caught a ride in one of the ambulances." Matias shrugged. "Thought I'd surprise you."

Giovanni hesitated, then shrugged. "Yeah, we do kinda need someone in the morgue. Just lay off the tidy-whitey and any other jokes!"

Matias just grinned as they pulled up to the old farmhouse they shared with two other roommates. It was old and decrepit, largely abandoned in a forgotten remnant of Georgia forest, but it was cheap. To his credit, Matias didn't say anything, but since his partner was hanging up his cell phone as they stepped into the dining room, he really didn't have to.

"Dude, I cannot believe you flashed the nurses - again!" Jeremy was laughing, but Giovanni wasn't sure if he was impressed or surprised. Then his expression changed to mild concern. "You really did a number on your legs though."

Giovanni looked down past the box he still carried at the red scrapes along his thighs. From a previous close encounter with a floor buffer, he knew he was in for muscle aches and stinging paresthesia as his skin healed. He sighed and looked for a place to put his load down.

"It's ridiculous." Cookie, coming out of the kitchen, was definitely unimpressed. "My buyer at the gift shop couldn't stop laughing."

Cookie had dark curly hair that bounced to her shoulders, an impression augmented by whatever shiny substance she used on it. In fact, shiny was pretty much the definition of her look as her clothes and nails and makeup all sparkled or contained sparkle or did something which made her hard to look at even in the weak artificial light of the basement. The sparkle in her eyes was completely undimmed, however.

"So that's good, right?" Matias wandered in from the hall. He yawned and slumped into a chair at the dining table. "You want people happy with your product. Or near your product anyway."

"Not when I'm trying to get her to increase the order!" Cookie huffed. She pivoted on one heel, then paused to peer at the box Giovanni carried in from the car.

"Another one! Jeeze, Gio, how many coffee makers do you need?" Cookie threw one hand in the general direction of the kitchen and rolled her eyes. "You've already got a regular coffee maker, a pod machine, Matias' espresso machine, and whatever that other thing is."

"That's a coffee press. It's better," Jeremy said just as Matias said, "yeah, but Gio's machine is better," and the two looked at each other in confusion.

Giovanni was amused by the exchange between the two men. Like most couples, they regularly finished each other's sentences, but since they didn't always agree, they didn't always get their words in sync. *But at least*, he added mentally, *I don't laugh out loud.*

Turning to the crowded kitchen countertop, Giovanni frowned at the impressive collection of coffee related appliances. He could see Cookie's point, but he was more concerned about the way she was behaving. It wasn't like Cookie to be critical. She was normally bouncy and bubbly and sometimes thoughtless, but seldom mean. Even when she skipped out on the rent, she seemed genuinely apologetic about it.

"This is the machine I lost my second semester, before I came to live with you guys. It's a nice one. My nonnas gave it to me for Christmas." Giovanni put the box down on the counter, angling it a little to squeeze it in with the other coffee machines. He gave it an affectionate pat and turned back to Cookie.

'So, what's your beef?" he asked.

"Oh God, no more gangster talk!" Cookie moaned. She dropped into a chair and laid her head on the table. Her glittery nail polish sparkled in the overhead lights as she wove her fingers through dark curls. "The gangsters are driving me nuts."

Giovanni frowned. "I thought we made it clear they were to leave you alone," he said. "Do you need me to get my cousin on them again?"

Cookie tilted her head, lips pursed as she considered his offer, and Giovanni tried not to feel jealous of the obvious interest his cousin Guido inspired in her. He might find Guido annoying and brash, but so far, Guido has been the only one to intimidate the gangsters ghosts accidentally called up last semester. Even Anthony, a retired sergeant as well as Mrs. Harris's nephew, had been unable to command their attention or cooperation.

"No," Cookie sighed. "They're not bothering me exactly. They even try to keep the noise down. It's just that someone always says something to hurt someone's feelings, then I've got flappers sniffling, trying not to bother me but bawling their heads off."

Giovanni exchanged a glance with Jeremy who shrugged.

"Why are the flappers upset?" Giovanni asked.

"Cause men are stupid and say mean things," Cookie mumbled from where she'd laid her head back down on the dining table.

Jeremy shook his head, both hands raised. "Not touching that."

Matias, returning from the kitchen, had a cup raised to his lips and sputtered as he tried to suppress a laugh. "So, without getting into gender discrimination, why don't you just ignore them?"

Cookie raised her head and glared at him. "Have you ever tried to ignore a sniffling flapper? They act so silly, but those guys are really mean to them. They just want a little respect!" Her earrings, also sparkly, swung from the momentum of her head bobbing and sent little flashes of light through the evening gloom creeping into the kitchen.

Matias hurriedly backtracked. "No, no, you don't want to be rude or unfeeling, but if they're interrupting your sleep –"

"I can't just ignore someone who's in pain!" Cookie cried out, and her voice hit a high-pitched note that made Matias wince.

Right behind her came another lower-pitched, yet still startling howl. All three roommates looked over at the chair, now toppled over, where Jeremy had been sitting. His place was now occupied by an enormous tan dog who snorted as it scrambled to his feet, drool spraying generously from his dangling jowls.

"Ew," Cookie said as Matias sighed.

"I have to get used to working late enough for moonrise now," he commented.

Giovanni almost started to repeat the information he'd gleaned over the past year about moon cycles but stopped as he realized that he hadn't changed into a dog. He'd started looking up moon cycles because the rougarou curse he'd caught in his first year of med school had routinely turned him into labradoodle, but now that curse seemed to have rebounded back onto the guy who originally gave it to him.

"Still nothing, huh?" Matias peered over at him wryly, then back at his partner who was now snuffling at the door that led from the dining room to the porch. "I'm mean, I'm happy for you and all, but why did the curse change? What brought it back?"

"Yeah," Cookie murmured, her gaze intent on the large mastiff. "It's not like he cheated this time."

Giovanni winced along with Matias, and both men turned to regard the large dog. Seeing he had their attention, the dog stopped his half-hearted whimper and went for a deep, full-throated bay.

"Okay, okay!" Matias hurried to let Jeremy out. "What's got you all riled up?"

Giovanni laughed, but his laughter faded as he followed Matias out onto the porch. Matias stood transfixed, grimly staring out into the backyard. Cookie gasped as she came out, then she too fell silent, riveted at the sight before them.

Jeremy growled as he ran outside, completely unlike his usual nearly somnambulant demeanor, but his mad dash outside didn't disturb the shadowy people in the back yard. A few gangsters, spectral in their grey suits, gestured towards the dog, but mostly they also stood and watched the phantoms that flickered in and out as they shuffled slowly across the tree line.

Staring at the wraiths, Giovanni swallowed hard. He'd seen all sorts of otherworldly phenomenon during his stint in medical school and even some real-life horrors, but nothing as profoundly disturbing. The men that traipsed across the backyard were broken, with terrific injuries that were a visual blow to anyone, not just the medically trained. Heads were wrapped in bleeding bandages, limbs dangled uselessly dragging across the ground, and gaping wounds were visible under ripped and filthy garments.

"Soldiers?" Matias asked softly.

"Yeah, Civil War, I think," Giovanni told him. He was silent for a moment, then reached out to touch Cookie on the shoulder. "They're just an illusion. It was over a long time ago," he told her.

Cookie looked at him strangely. "Obviously not," she said and went back into the house.

"They're real alright." One of the gangsters drifted closer to him, a translucent tommy gun resting casually on one shoulder. "Those palookas woke up from the deep sleep and just cause they ain't belching don't mean they're happy."

"Hi, Jimmy," Giovanni sighed. The portly gangster had returned to the old house that had been his speakeasy along with his mob after a Halloween party the roommates threw got out of control. All things considered, Giovanni would have preferred an irate landlord, but he liked the old gangster anyway.

"This dance hall's a gyp." Jimmy told him and sounded worried. "You gotta get them round the horn pronto, Gio. This ain't on the up and up. You throwing the boots in." The gangster threw him a look as heavily meaty as his transparent bulk would have been pre-death.

Giovanni swallowed hard. Jimmy was intimidating, even translucent and besides, he was right. Calling up these ghosts was cruel. They didn't need to relive the prolonged agony of dying from their wounds again. It hurt to look at them. And the memories they brought flooding back hurt. Of all the monsters he'd encountered, from werewolves to vampires, the ghosts and the realizations of lives lost were the horrors that hurt the most. Add that pain to the ache of responsibility he felt over Mrs. Harris, and he felt a tiredness that made even double shifts feel less exhausting.

"I know," he told Jimmy the Gent. "I'll get on it. I will, just as soon as I figure out how."

Matias clapped him on one shoulder. "Dude, you cannot do this by yourself.

"Okay, then," Giovanni turned on him. "What do you suggest?

Matias shook his head. "You gotta call Mama Nene."

Giovanni winced at the thought of reaching out to the elderly voodoo mambo. The last time they'd seen her was the out-of-control party that called up the gangster ghosts. She'd not been happy about that. "She said it was our mess. We would have to deal with it."

Matias watched the slowly shuffling troops in the back yard and sighed. "Dude, I will be the first to take the blame. But face it, we are in deep shit. You cannot be a hero. Beg if you have to."

Giovanni sighed. Ms. Suarez, her sister, Mrs. Harris, the gangsters, and now soldiers – the losses and lost surrounding him were starting to pile up. "Yeah," he said. "On it."

Chapter 5

Mama Nene's house was not what Giovanni expected. Somehow, he'd pictured a quiet place, white with a tower maybe – okay he'd pictured a church. But Mama Nene lived in a plain frame house that could use some paint. Pretty rose bushes were planted beside the front door, but the yard was plain dirt that routinely hosted heavy vehicles judging from the tire tracks left behind in long stripes.

The woman who opened the door didn't look any happier to see Giovanni than he was to be there. Rolling her eyes, she stepped back to let him in.

"You were right," she called as she headed down a dark hallway. "It's that college boy."

Following, Giovanni saw an elderly woman, tiny in an overstuffed recliner, regarding him intently. The room was cluttered with knickknacks on small tables and shelves, rather like the house he shared before he and his roommates had hauled all the extra furniture out to the shed to make room for the TV. There was no TV in Mama Nene's living room and Giovanni suspected not in her house.

What there was, however, was a great snake, twisting lazily in a giant glass box that doubled as a coffee table in front of the little, old wizen woman in her oversized lounger. The snake's tongue flickered, and Giovanni would have sworn the thing was blowing him a raspberry. Well, he wasn't too fond of Le Grand Zombie either after the thing made him look bad in front of his supervising physician the first time he'd met Mama Nene.

"Good morning," Giovanni started in his most professional voice, but stopped abruptly as he realized he hadn't really thought out what he wanted to say.

Mama Nene just grinned at him, so Giovanni took a deep breath. The room smelled musty, not in an old lady, baby powder way, but with a faint lingering odor of earth and cut flowers wilting. The snake lay on a bedding of mulch and what appeared to be old towels which explained some of the earthy smell. And while Giovanni couldn't see any vases among the clutter in the living room, he could see bunches of cut vegetation hanging to dry in the kitchen on the other side of the hall.

Trying again, Giovanni said, "Thank you for seeing me. I was hoping I could consult with you on…" and he hesitated, not sure exactly what the right term for his troubles was.

The woman who had let him in snorted. She was standing not terribly unobtrusively near a sliding glass door that led to the back yard, pretending to dust overcrowded shelves. Giovanni could see another of Mama Nene's acolytes, also dressed in white, wielding a garden hose over extensive and thriving vegetable plots. The man outside looked up and waved, his white clothes startling in the early spring sun, weak as it was.

Seeing the white garments, Giovanni remembered that Mama Nene was the head of a large and powerful voodoo house, one that intervened once before to save him from a terrifying voodoo curse. Well, actually they'd just confirmed the voodoo curse, but they'd revealed the culprit, so – suddenly overwhelmed, Giovanni dropped into a nearby armchair.

"Oh hell, we are so screwed, and I have no idea what to about it," he said.

Mama Nene laughed, a high-pitched wheeze that bounced around the cluttered living room and up against the glass sliding doors. Inside its glass casket, the snake rippled into new coils. Hunching forward, Mama Nene peered at Giovanni, one eyebrow rising higher on her weathered face. "Didn't I tell you to not mess around? You fool with things you don't know, you're gonna get trouble!"

Giovanni heard the woman near the patio door humphed loudly, but he ignored her and instead watched Mama Nene hopefully.

"I know, I know," he said, "But we really were trying to help. We were trying to find Mrs. Harris."

"You were having a party," Mama Nene replied bluntly.

Giovanni sighed. "Okay, yeah, but we were also trying to find Mrs. Harris. We just weren't any good at it, and now we've got ghosts."

Mama Nene shrugged, a broadly expansive gesture that consumed most of her tiny body. It reminded Giovanni uncomfortably of the way the snake moved. "You called them up. You must deal with them."

"Well, yeah," Giovanni tried to explain. "The gangsters aren't so bad, well Cookie doesn't like them, but the Civil War ghosts don't even speak."

"Wait, wait," came an excited squeak from the duster. "You've got more ghosts?"

"Uh-huh," Giovanni turned to the priestess, nodding earnestly. "They just showed up in the backyard. We didn't call them or anything."

The priestess scurried into a chair near Giovanni, still clutching her duster. "You're sure?" she asked. "No chanting, jokes? Didn't light candles, make a casual wish?"

"No!" Giovanni protested. "I wasn't even there. I just got home from work, I set my espresso machine down on the counter, and suddenly there they were!"

But –" the priestess started, but Mama Nene waved her to a stop with a sharp gesture and almost guttural puff of air through tensed lips. Mama Nene seemed to be listening intently, her gaze fixed somewhere between Giovanni and the priestess. In its glass coffin, the snake froze in the intent stillness only apex predators can pull off.

"You said nothing? You did nothing?" Mama Nene asked eventually. She frowned so deeply, her forehead looked like a craggy cliff face ready to fall.

"Nothing," Giovanni whispered. "I came in, I talked to Cookie, it got dark. Jeremy turned into a dog and went barking after the ghosts. New ones in the back yard from the Civil War." He swallowed hard remembering the broken lurching bodies that had appeared and feeling a little sick at the memory.

"You did not turn?" Mama Nene barked at him. "You no longer carry the rougaroo curse?"

Giovanni shook his head and Mama Nene settled back into her recliner, face still wrinkled in deep thought.

"That is interesting," the high priestess mused. "With all the supermoons and full moons combined, he should still be feeling some effect."

"I read about that," Giovanni agreed. "That we're supposed to have full moons and supermoons for the next decade and the new ones will be full. I think. I didn't quite follow the math."

Mama Nene quirked one eyebrow, her mouth twisting. "And yet, you don't change. The power is going somewhere else."

"Well, Jeremy," Giovanni started, but Mama Nene shook her head.

"Rougaroo is a powerful curse," the high priestess started, but Mama Nene shushed her.

"You weren't carrying anything?" the priestess whispered to Giovanni. "You didn't pick up anything, maybe one of Astral's gris-gris?"

"God no, Astral would kill me if I touched her stuff." Giovanni shuddered a little at the memory of his former roommate. He'd run afoul of one of her curses, and she hadn't even been aiming it at him.

The priestess nodded in agreement, but almost absently, as if her thoughts were elsewhere. Giovanni debated internally for a moment about breaking the contemplative silence, then couldn't hold back any longer.

"Speaking of Astral," he began, "we were wondering if you'd heard of any bokors lately?

Mama Nene drew back abruptly. "Are you calling one of my congregation a bokor?" she demanded, clearly offended.

"Serving the lwa is our right," the priestess added, bouncing to the edge of her seat.

"No, no," Giovanni scrambled to explain. "I just meant maybe somebody confused about voodoo, like Astral. Maybe somebody practicing without a license."

He winced inwardly at his lame excuse and at the exchange of arched eyebrows between the two women, but honestly, Astral had caused a lot of trouble before she started training with Mama Nene. Considering she'd manage to curse both Jeremy and then Giovanni, Astral had been working through a lot of anger, even if that last part had been an accident. Mama Nene had addressed that too, much like Giovanni's nonnas would though probably not with the same wooden spoon.

"No," the priestess said, decisive and settling back into her chair. "If there was a bokor around, we would know about it."

Giovanni sighed. "Well, that's what Astral said, only we can't think of any other reason for grabbing Mrs. H. There was no ransom note, nothing. You know the vampires would have made demands."

Mama Nene nodded. Everyone knew vampires were out for everything they could get. They'd taken over the campus coffee shops at the end of last year, and students had not only lost out on valuable study time, but they'd also lost cash, laptops, cell phones, jewelry, and what little credit college students managed to hold on to after taking out student loans. The vampires wouldn't have missed a chance to make money in some way, so they had to be compensated by somebody.

The priestess frowned. "Are you sure you didn't do anything different, anything out of the ordinary?"

"No," Giovanni replied. "The only new thing we found was my old espresso machine. Well, it's still new. I never used it. I lost in my second semester, but there it was in the sub-basement."

"You shouldn't drink coffee," Mama Nene and the priestess chorused. Mama Nene added, "Coffee is a stimulant" in the same tone his nonnas would have declare something a sin.

Giovanni wasn't listening though. "You know there was something weird about the sub-basement," he said musing aloud to himself. "All those biological hazard boxes."

"You work in the morgue. You don't have biological hazards?" The priestess looked exasperated.

Giovanni caught her expression and blushed. "It's just that the sub-basement is storage. You would have boxes of containment bags and labels, but boxes themselves take up too much room. Any boxes would be broken down until you needed them."

"Break down?" Mama Nene looked confused. "Who is having a breakdown?"

Me, though Giovanni as the priestess said, "He means boxes that aren't assembled. You know, the flat ones you have to open up and seal before using."

"They could just be mislabeled, but I don't remember. I'd have to check." Giovanni noticed the baffled exchange between the two voodoo mambos and added, "It's the only odd thing I can think of."

Mama Nene nodded decisively. "Okay, you go check that out. We're gonna trace the power from your house."

"Really? Cool!" Having seen her in action, Giovanni had no doubt Mama Nene could do that. And at this point, he didn't care what she did. He was just happy to have her back on their side. It was such a relief to not be alone dealing with ghosts, it felt almost physical, like the rush of waves at the beach, practically sensual. He would have jumped or danced if he'd been in his own living room.

"Yeah, yeah." The priestess said what Mama Nene was probably thinking but was too polite to say. "This doesn't mean you get to fool around with the *regleman.* Voodoo is not a game."

"One more time," Mama Nene's deep voice broke across the priestess's scolding. Inside his glass sarcophagus, the snake twisted lazily. "One more time. You will have to lay Mrs. Harris to rest."

"But she's... I mean, there's nothing to bury," Giovanni said. "She was just a ghost the last time I saw her."

"Yes," Mama Nene agreed. "Since the *dessounin* wasn't completed when she died, *la petit ange* is untethered. We need to find her and complete the regleman."

Giovanni wasn't entirely sure what Mama Nene was talking about, but her heard the regret in her voice. "It's not your fault," he started, "we didn't even know you then..."

"*Ti bon ange* is the part of the soul that is the person," the high priestess explained. "It's the life experiences, the knowledge, and it must be protected. The ti bon ange must be separated from the body and preserved, so it can pass on to *Les Invisibles* and become one of the ancestral spirits."

Giovanni regarded her blankly. Sighing, the priestess added, "Without the regleman, the ti bon ange can become *zonbi lastral*. She could be trapped and used by a bokor as you said or just wander the world, random energy causing who knows what sort of mischief."

Giovanni sighed. That he understood. Random mischief perfectly described Mrs. Harris. And if performing another voodoo ritual kept her safe and happy, then he was all for it. It was the least he could do.

"What about Anthony?" he said. "He's her nephew. Can he find her and help?"

"She came to you," Mama Nene replied. "You will have to help her pass."

She sank back into her chair and regarded him steadily. Sobered and once again overwhelmed by responsibility, Giovanni gulped and simply nodded.

Chapter 6

With Mama Nene's directive ringing in his ears, Giovanni was determined to follow up on his suspicions about the sub-basement, but school and career intervened first. It was funny how when he was just a student, he ran around all hours between the hospital, but now that he had more or less regular hours doing rotations, he felt like he could sleep around the clock. It was getting harder and harder to study nights in the morgue, but he had no choice.

He might not have regular labs anymore, but now he had the second level of the Boards to pass and real people to diagnose. When he hit the end of an eight-hour day, he couldn't just chuck the endless redirects from the insurance companies and go home for dinner. Or in Giovanni's case, back to the cafeteria to pick up something to take down to the morgue.

He'd just worked his way to the bottom of one stack and was reaching for another when his pager buzzed. It startled him, used as he was to hearing his phone chime, and he had to fumble for it before it went off a second time. Old-school as it might seem, the hospital was strict about using pagers as that system was more reliable in emergencies than cell phones. Glancing at it, Giovanni read,

"RQSTD RTM: SUAREZ 54 F Origin Unit: EMS Admitting: PATEL Level of Care: 1st Avail Medical Diagnosis: RESP_ARREST TIME: 18:43:29 Disp: E2"

Giovanni hesitated only a minute. Requested recall team member might not apply to him, but the name Suarez jumped out at him. That was the name of the nice lady with bossy sister he'd met just days earlier. The more he thought about it, remembering the pleasant Margie and the cranky Rita, the more his anxiety grew until he jumped up and hurried out, leaving the stacks of paper scattered behind him.

The emergency room was the usual level of subdued chaos, everybody trying to be quiet and thoughtful of the patients who needed immediate, even urgent care. The ICU, however, which normally maintained an almost militant calm, had a number of people moving up and down the corridor in understated frenzy. Spotting Dr. Patel in conference with several nurses, Giovanni hurried over.

"Oh, good." Dr. Patel looked up even as he moved away. "Giovanni, I need you to take of Mrs. Hernandez. Her sister, Margie's, back with labored breathing, irregular pulse–" He broke off to take a tablet from an arriving nurse.

"Why? What's going on?" Giovanni started, but another nurse caught him by the elbow and pulled him away.

"It's not good," she told him. "We need you to keep the sister calm. We'll let you know as soon as we know."

"Right, right." Giovanni nodded and then, realizing what he'd probably be asked, panicked. After all, he'd only met the woman once, and she yelled at him then.

"What should I tell her?" he asked the nurse, wide-eyed.

The nurse gave him a gentle push. "You know her, she knows you. Help her out."

Taking a deep breath, Giovanni headed to the ICU waiting room. "Uh, Mrs. Hernandez?"

The middle-aged woman he remembered from his early encounter sat alone even though there were other people in the room. She perched on the edge of her seat, nervously flexing one hand. The other clenched a phone tightly enough that her fingers were white. When she looked up, her face was pale and her eyes shiny with tears.

A rush of sympathy swept over Giovanni at the sight of her obvious pain. Sitting down beside her, he asked, "Aren't any of your family here?" and immediately wished he hadn't.

Mrs. Hernandez started to speak, swallowed hard, then said, "My kids are at school. I have to go get them, but I can't –" Her mouth twisted tight as she broke off speaking.

"Can you call them?" Giovanni started.

Mrs. Hernandez lifted on hand helplessly, and Giovanni hurried to say, "No, no, maybe text them?"

"I don't know what to say," Mrs. Hernandez managed. "I can't leave."

"No." Giovanni thought fast. "Can they go home with friends maybe? That would be good. They'd have someone to stay with."

Mrs. Hernandez nodded and fumbled with the small plastic rectangle she held as tightly as any lifeline.

"Here, I'll help," Giovanni offered, taking the phone. "Just show me their contact. That's it."

Thumbs moving rapidly over the small keyboard, Giovanni typed a brief announcement and instructions to Mrs. Hernandez' kids, waiting for her to nod approval before hitting send. Then he handed back the phone and sat awkwardly and silent, not sure what else he could say or do to help more. Casting about uselessly in his mind, Giovanni would have given almost anything for a new topic to address.

"She's not going to make it, is she?' Mrs. Hernandez asked suddenly.

Caught off guard, Giovanni could only gape at the woman sitting next to him. Mrs. Hernandez didn't return his gaze but started intently at the air immediately in front of her, her attention entirely elsewhere.

"She got worse so fast," Mrs. Hernandez said, almost astonished. "We were just talking about having lunch and when I looked back, she'd just sort of collapsed. I mean, I was just in the kitchen and when I looked back, she'd slumped over on the sofa."

She turned to regard Giovanni, eyes wide and baffled. "All I could do was call 9-1-1. We were just talking."

Giovanni felt his throat grow tight and had trouble breathing. He managed a nod and replied in a tight voice, "You did the right thing."

"I really thought she was getting better," Mrs. Hernandez said in a tight, small voice, and the tears spilled over to run down her cheeks.

Giovanni reached over and took her hand. "It's okay," he choked out. "They're gonna do everything they can."

"I don't know whether to be relieved or sad," Mrs. Hernandez continued. "She really hated that feeding tube."

Giovanni started to say something about switching to a PEG tube, but he could feel the tears starting and his throat closing up, so when Mrs. Hernandez pulled him in for a hug, he, of course, bawled like a baby.

"It's okay. It's okay," Mrs. Hernandez crooned. "We'll get through it."

Giovanni would have liked to have pulled himself together, but by the time Dr. Patel came to find him and Mrs. Hernandez, he'd only managed to cry himself out. He and Mrs. Hernandez sat side by side, sniffling softly but no longer crying. Giovanni was so exhausted, his face hurt, and his head was pounding. He couldn't breathe except though his mouth, he was so congested, and his heart hurt so much over Mrs. Hernandez's loss, any thought threatened to start him crying all over again. He couldn't even imagine what she felt.

Dr. Patel looked at him strangely but turned his attention to Mrs. Hernandez. Taking her hand, he said, "I am so sorry. We did everything we could, but sometimes it's just too much for the body to handle."

Mrs. Hernandez didn't return his gaze but nodded. "Now I've got to pay for the funeral," she said.

"I can help with that." Giovanni dug through his backpack for the list of approved funeral homes he'd been checking the morgue discharge forms against. "These are the funeral homes the hospital works with regularly. You can tell them we sent you."

He held out the sheet of paper to Mrs. Hernandez who took it with a weak smile. "Thank you," she said and hugged Giovanni fiercely once again.

"I'll take you to see your sister if you'd like," Dr Patel added and gently led Mrs. Hernandez away.

Giovanni turned his body away from the room in a futile attempt to hide the tears that had started fresh and found himself face-to-face with the duty nurse.

"Sorry," he managed. "I didn't answer very many questions."

The duty nurse smiled sadly. "It's good that you listened. Go get cleaned up, tidy whitey guy. The patient advocate is on their way."

Too tired to even argue, Giovanni headed first to the bathroom where he splashed cold water across his swollen eyes, then down to the morgue where he hoped he could be alone. He didn't think he could handle the staff room with any sympathetic looks or queries from his peers. At least in the morgue, he could run off any students and just sit quietly for a moment.

He wasn't entirely surprised to find the morgue empty as it was growing late, but for a moment, he was angry. What was it going to take to get the students to take their shifts seriously? The morgue should never be left unattended. Then already spent, he dropped into a chair and merely thought again that they badly needed a new morgue manager. For a minute, he wondered if Mr. Lively was the patient advocate hurrying to Mrs. Hernandez' side, then the sorrow he'd tried to squash came flooding back and overwhelmed him.

His mind kept skittering away from the thought of Mrs. Suarez passing. He knew it could happen, he'd just witnessed it, but there was this frightening, gaping void when he thought of her as just gone. The thought left him breathless, reeling way from the same desolation he'd seen in Mrs. Hernandez's face. He'd had to look away from her shock and pain lest they both teeter over the edge of some yawning gulf.

And now safe in the morgue, no longer nodding and grimacing through the polite motions, the accepted social response, he still felt hollow, gutted, as he sat numb, momentarily dry-eyed, in a kind of shock without visible hysterics, but silent, screaming rejection raging inside.

Chapter 7

When the elevator chimed, Giovanni jumped up and ran for the paper towels on the counter across the back of the office. Hastily wiping at his eyes, he called out, "Who's there?"

"Hello to you too," Fred grumbled. The elderly orderly maneuvered his bulk into the morgue, hunched over the plastic tray he was carrying. Visible steam rose from the plates on it, a faint smell of chicken and potatoes drifting out.

"Wait, wha...?" Giovanni stared as the old man carefully arranged the plates on a desk. He then stood back and waved one hand towards the chair as Giovanni stood blinking stupidly.

"You brought me dinner?"

"You need more vegetables," Fred barked at him. "Here," and he slapped a serving of something green onto the desk.

"Sorry," said Giovanni. "What is that?"

"Collard greens. You'll like them. They're spicy, like spinach."

Giovanni regarded the vegetables dubiously.

Fred pulled an apple out of one pocket. "Take this for latter. You gotta be clean for the regleman. You need to start eating healthy. No more coffee."

Giovanni almost groaned out loud. Still if no coffee would help him find Mrs. Harris, then no coffee it was. It wasn't like he ever finished the cup anymore, so it was probably more economical anyway. Giovanni sighed.

"Sit, eat," Fred rumbled and nudged the chair towards Giovanni.

Giovanni sat down and picked up the fork Fred held out to him. The old man sighed heavily as he settled into a second office chair.

"Collard greens can be tough, but the cafeteria ladies do all right with them." Fred leaned back in his chair and folded his arms, so they rested on the substantial bulk of his stomach. "See the secret to greens is to slow cook them, get all the bitterness out. The ladies let them sit on a burner all day. Good for greens, bad for spinach." Fred pinched his bridge of his nose between two thick fingers and shook his head. "What those ladies do to spinach!"

"You were a cook?" Giovanni mumbled around a bite of chicken. It was salty, but hot and juicy and comforting as he swallowed.

"Here and there," Fred told him. "Here and there. Eat your greens."

Giovanni obediently forked up some of the vegetables and swallowed them hastily. They weren't bad, but tart. They were warm sliding down his throat though, soothing his feelings as well as his esophagus.

"I thought you were a roadie for Wilson Picket," he mumbled around a mouthful of potatoes.

"More greens," Fred told him, thumping a thick finger against the desktop.

"You said you knew The Who," Giovanni persisted as he shoveled more greens onto his fork. "Back when we first met, when I ended up cursed." And he grimaced at the memory.

"I remember," Fred rumbled. He peered fiercely at Giovanni, brows knitting. "That was in '67." A sudden grin lightened his face. "Crazy, man, the way they smashed their instruments. Ruining perfectly good guitars."

"Picket didn't like that?" Giovanni asked.

"He didn't like the smoke." Fred leaned back in his chair and fumbled in one pocket, pulling out an apple. Taking a bite, he mumbled. "They weren't bad though. Had a good vibe. And they were headed to California, so I tagged along. Went to the Monterey International Pop Festival."

"Really?" Giovanni grinned at the thought of the elderly man as a teenager hippie. Despite the man's bulk and white hair, he still had a youthful intensity about him, the single-mindedness of a younger man. "Then you saw Jimi Hendricks perform."

"Oh yeah," Fred said. "Amazing. That was my last concert though."

Giovanni blinked as Fred shrugged. "Got hurt. Fell from the scaffolding, so couldn't be a roadie anymore."

"I'm sorry," Giovanni said. It seemed an inadequate response considering what a cool opportunity Fred h ad given up.

"S' okay." Fred shrugged. "I stayed on in San Francisco. I loved the beach, warmer than Detroit, less humid than Memphis." And he grinned.

"So, you just hung out at the beach then, became a hippie?"

"Nah." Fred shifted in his chair. He didn't look at Giovanni, his thoughts seeming far away.

"The Black Panthers had just started up in Oakland, cop-watching," he said. "They get a bad rap now, but they saved me. They saved a lot of people."

Giovanni waited, trying to breath softly so he wouldn't interrupt the old man's musing.

"I had a busted leg, couldn't work, no place to go. The Panthers had a community health clinic and free breakfast for kids. They literally kept me going. Once I could move around again, I helped out. Worked with the free breakfast program, helped out other shut-ins. That's how I got involved with hospitals."

Kids? Giovanni thought and wondered how young a teenager Fred had been. What he asked though was, "This hospital?" and wondered how Fred had gotten from San Francisco to Atlanta.

"Not this one." Fred looked scornful. "That came later. I got to know some people in San Francisco 'cause I was helping this handicapped guy get back and forth to the hospital. See, Medicare had only just started, but veterans had medical since WWII. He could see a doctor, but he needed help to get there. That was me."

Fred shifted again in his chair, his bulk making the aluminum frame squeak. "Met a lot of guys, and some gals too, who were in wheelchairs. They had a tough time. None of the stuff we have today, no ramps, lifts on the busses, nothing. There'd been laws passed, but the Health and Education Welfare department dragged around so much implementing them, finally people started protesting."

"Really?" Giovanni asked weakly. He wasn't sure he wanted to know how Fred had protested with the Blank Panthers.

"Uh-huh, we provided daily home-cooked meals to support the 504 Sit-In at the San Francisco Federal Building. Over a hundred people occupied the building for nearly a month, wheelchairs blocking corridors, people bathing in sinks, people sleeping anywhere they could. The powers that be learned exactly how inaccessible that building was!" Fred laughed. "Eventually the HEW signed off on the necessary regs for the Rehab Act of '73. Nondiscrimination became a right."

"Cool!" Giovanni smiled at the sight of Fred remembering that triumph. "So how did you end up working for, um, the Illuminati?"

"The clue is in the title. illuminati, illuminate, shine the light?" Fred hummed as he spoke, and Giovanni could hear Elton John singing *Philadelphia Freedom* in his head. Fred grinned at him as if he knew what Giovanni was thinking.

"We're not some weird religious group with dumb rituals, just a bunch of people who've seen the light and try to keep it going," Fred went on.

Giovanni frowned and shook his head confused. Fred sighed.

"Hospitals are transition places," he explained. "Babies are born, people die." He shrugged. "You see things, things that need to be taken care of, you get to know other people who take care of things. Same as in any organization. After a while, word spreads about who can take care of what."

He lifted both hands and spread them wide in a shrug. "Here I am."

Giovanni laughed, then sobered. "Why are you telling me this?"

Fred shrugged. "Did you learn anything?"

"Sometimes things work out?" Giovanni suggested weakly.

"Sometimes," Fred agreed.

Giovanni sighed. "I don't know why this is bothering me so much, Mrs. Suarez's passing. I barely knew her. It's just..." and he swallowed hard as tears threatened to overwhelm him again.

"Have you ever lost anyone before?" Fred's deep voice was bland, almost distant, but very calming. For a minute, he sounded remarkably like Dr. Beverly, only a bass, not a contralto.

Shaking off the tears, Giovanni answered, "No, not really. Not unless you count Mrs. H., but I lost her twice."

"That doesn't count." A new voice came from the hall. "She's still around. We just have to find her."

Mattias walked in and grasped Giovanni's shoulder. Jeremy followed him with Cookie on his heels. "Your floor nurse called down to the Emergency Room. Thought you could use someone to talk to."

"Then Matias told me, and I told Cookie." Jeremy reached over and hugged him. "You gonna be okay, Gio," Jeremy said, his voice unexpectedly gruff.

Cookie didn't say anything, just smiled at him which had him blinking back tears again.

Sniffling, he turned to Matias. "I don't know why this is affecting me so."

"Hey, sooner or later, there's a case that just to gets to you," Matias said, and Giovanni remembered that Matias was an EMT and had seen more than his share of loss as well.

The elevator chimed, and everyone turned to see who was coming down the hall. Tall and blond, Huntington stumbled when he saw all eyes on him. The girl next to him, clutching his arm, giggled as she staggered too. Giovanni almost smirked at the thought of the handsome man tripping. It was an uncharitable thought, but Huntington's looks were an unfair advantage. Certainly, the women standing next to him thought he was adorable. Betty Kyung stared up at him, lips parted slightly, one hand stroking her long dark hair. *Well, she was always touching her hair,* Giovanni thought. It was like her pet. Cookie, however, wasn't madly in love with Huntington, a thought which Giovanni found very comforting.

"Hi, Betty," Cookie greeted her friend.

"I heard you lost a patient," Huntington said to Giovanni. "Sorry, man."

Giovanni nodded but couldn't get out any words. Huntington patted him on the shoulder.

"Well, if we all gonna hang out in the morgue, we should probably order pizza or something," Cookie said.

Fred winced and shook his head. Giovanni took another bite of his greens which weren't as good now that they were getting cold.

"No, no," Jeremy interjected. "We need to check out this sub-basement and look for Mrs. H."

"We already did that," Giovanni started as Fred rumbled, "You guys stay out of the sub-basement."

"We just thought we might see something you missed," Matias told both Fred and Giovanni, his head swiveling between them. "There's got to be more down there than a coffee maker."

"Espresso machine," Giovanni responded automatically, ignoring the slight. "There was something weird about those supplies."

"See," Jeremy added. "Let's go check them out."

"Uh-uh!" Cookie drew back. "The heroine always gets it in the basement."

"We're already in the basement," Huntington said as Betty added, "It's usually a blond though."

"You can go first," Jeremy told Huntington.

Huntington took one step out into the hall, then stopped frowning. "Wait a minute," he said as Matias ducked his head to hide his smile, but Jeremy grinned openly.

"I'll go." Betty tossed her hair and scooted past the tall resident.

"Even better," Jeremey added. Everyone turned to look askance at him.

"What?" Jeremy asked. "She's got a black belt."

"That's true," Betty glared at Jeremy. "As long as you don't assume!"

Jeremy made a face and stepped back to let her pass.

"Wait a minute!" Huntington put out one hand to stop Betty. "I'm going first."

"Oh, for Pete's sake!" Giovanni exclaimed impatiently. "We'll all go. It's just boxes downstairs."

Still, he stepped hesitantly down the emergency stairwell, followed closely by his friends. In fact, he nearly elbowed Jeremy as he eased the sub-basement door open. Spooked, he snapped, "What are you doing?"

"Dude," Jeremy hissed. "I'm practically your dog. I can't let you go by yourself."

Seeing Matias right behind him, Giovanni asked, "And you're here because...?"

"I'm here to keep an eye on Captain Courageous."

"Oh, please," Cookie added from further behind him. "Like you guys could manage without me."

"Get on with it!" roared Fred from the end of the line.

Giovanni managed to get the door open, and the lot of them stumbled inside to stand blinking at the banks of stockpiled supplies.

"See," Huntington said, waving at the boxes surrounding them. "There's nothing here. Just stuff."

"Yeah, it's all supplies for an emergency, except...." Giovanni paused to pull a carton towards him on the shelf and peer at it closely.

"Matias," he asked. "Is this storage for biological samples?"

"Hazardous waste," Jeremy read the red warning label. "Why would you store hazardous waste?"

"It's packing material, so you can safely contain hazardous waste. Like the red garbage bags we use up in the ER and operating rooms," Fred told them. "Stop poking around now."

"Yeah," Cookie chimed in. "You've seen everything. Let's go."

"No, wait!" Matias' voice echoed from where he'd wandered deeper into the rows of shelves that crowded the sub-basement. "These aren't packaging. These are biological samples!"

Chapter 8

Giovanni exchanged a startled look with Huntington and hurried over to where Matias wrestled with a cooler. He'd pulled a box off one of the shelves and now struggled to slide the cooler out of the box.

"See," he managed, a bit breathless, as both men drew closer, "these aren't the original boxes. Or not the original contents. Anyway, you can see that they don't hold packing supplies."

"What's in it?" Betty asked, horror tinged with fascination in her voice.

"It's okay," Huntington said, his voice deepening as he dropped one hand on her shoulder.

Betty and Cookie exchanged a look that, fortunately, Huntington didn't see.

"Well, don't open it here," Fred barked. "We'll take it upstairs where we can call Administration if necessary."

"Check to see if there's anything else out of place before we go," Jeremy said.

Everyone looked around, heads shaking as they observed the piles of boxes.

"What about the coffee press?" Jeremy persisted.

Giovanni turned to the jumble of glassware on the low counter across the back of the room. "Nah, that's just junk," he said and reached out to touch the slender vase.

A wave of dizziness swept over him, leaving him clutching the countertop. He hadn't felt this ill since that time he'd had to deal with Mrs. Harris' rotting corpse as she sat scolding him in the morgue office, leaking body fluids everywhere. Man, he'd been glad when she could leave her body behind, a desiccated skeleton up in the Blue Ridge Mountains. She'd been even happier when that had happened, a veritable effervescent fountain of joy. He could feel that laughter bubbling up inside him, or no, maybe that was nausea, but then a wave of sorrow hit him, regret so deep and profound, he found himself leaning on the countertop and weeping.

"What the hell?" Matias abandoned his cooler and came over to wrap his arms around Giovanni. "It's okay, man, it'll be okay."

"Gio, look at me," Cookie demanded. "What's wrong? What's going on?"

"It's just a coffee press," Jeremy added, reaching for the tall, slender column of glass.

"Don't touch that!" Giovanni managed. He took a deep, gulping breath. "I think... I think it's Mrs. H."

Jeremy pulled his hand away quickly and stepped back.

"Nobody touch anything," Fred commanded. "We gotta get it upstairs to examine it. One of you find a box or lid or something we can carry it in."

Huntington nodded and turned back to the stacks, but Betty just pulled off her jacket and offered it to the elderly orderly. Nodding his thanks, Fred carefully reached out with his hands wrapped in folds of quilted nylon and lifted the glass beaker.

"Okay," he said when he had the elongated jar firmly in hand. "Everyone upstairs. Don't forget the cooler."

Giovanni trailed after the group, fragments of their conversation drifting back to him in hushed whispers. He felt better as Fred pulled ahead, but the wash of emotions he'd experienced left him disoriented and stumbling.

Cookie held back to wait for him. "You really think it's Mrs. H?"

Giovanni nodded, happy to stop and focus on her. "It felt like her, all happy and sad all at once. Just really strong, all of it at once, all over the place."

Cookie pursed her lips. "That sounds like Mrs. H. Don't let it get to you. We're gonna send her back as soon as possible, so it'll be alright."

Giovanni nodded. "I hope so. I don't know if she'll go, but," and he waved one hand vaguely, "this can't be good."

"C'mon." Cookie took his hand and pulled Giovanni after the others.

Upstairs, they found Matias studying the cooler he'd set on one desk, while Fred examined the coffee press now resting on the back counter of the morgue office. Jeremy stood with Fred, but turned excitedly as Giovanni came in.

"Gio, look at this. I think you're right. I think we've found her."

As Fred moved down the counter to make room for Giovanni, the overhead lights caught and glinted off something in the glass carafe. Bright reflections bounced crazily around the room for a second, so fast that Giovanni almost thought he imagined it. But then, the thick liquid inside the decanter shifted and send light spinning once again, so the whole thing seemed filled with a living viscosity, a life force revealed in restless movement.

"That's not soapy water," Giovanni breathed.

"Nope," Fred agreed. "Don't know what it is, but what it's holding is your Mrs. Harris, I think. Her *ti bon ange* is in there."

"Huh, that's funny," a new voice commented. "I wondered what that was."

Giovanni jumped, then turned to see the student whose homework he'd pitched out as an object lesson to the freshman class assigned to the morgue. "What was what?" Giovanni snapped.

"Ti bon ange. What you said. I thought it was Bon Angie, you know like Angie's List. I didn't know how it was pronounced." The student tilted his head to regard the coffee press. "What is that... a kind of dish soap?" How do they get it sparkly like that?"

"Never you mind," Fred told him even as Giovanni asked, "Where did you hear that name?"

The student blinked from one to the other man confronting him and unconsciously straightened up to his full, albeit rather skinny height. "Um, you said, well he said, to check out these companies and uh, that's what one of them's named."

Giovanni grabbed the sheaf of papers the student held out and recognized the incomplete routing forms he'd collected when he force-cleaned the morgue. Part of his mind noted that the morgue had remained clean, which was good, but the majority of his attention was focused on the puzzling paperwork. "So, you're saying these bodies were released to a company called Ti Bon Ange."

"Yeah," the student confirmed. "It's a charity. They do free cremations and stuff if you donate the body to science."

"That ain't right," Fred rumbled. "Donations go upstairs through Administration. They don't come down here for someone else to haul them off."

"We have a problem." Matias came over to the group at the counter.

Fred sighed and passed one hand over his face before pointedly raising his eyebrows in Matias's direction.

Matias gestured back toward the cooler set on one desk. "According to the label, that contains body parts. A hand and a foot to be exact."

"Did you open it?" Huntington bent over to peer at the cooler.

"No!" Fred exclaimed. "Don't be opening that. We can't be releasing lord know what all over the place."

"It's sealed," Matias added. "But what's really weird is that it's cold."

The group looked at him blankly.

"Well, how can it be cold?" he asked. "Even dry ice isn't going to last more than twenty-four hours, and this has been sitting in storage."

"Well, we don't know how long it's been in storage…" Jeremy started.

"There was dust on the box, and this is a sealed container. If it did have dry ice in it, the sublimates would have made it explode." Matias frowned at the cooler. "This is not a good storage solution."

"No," Giovanni and Huntington agreed together. They exchanged a startled glance even as Fred rolled his eyes.

"It's not procedure," Giovanni started, but was interrupted.

"I can get rid of it for you if you'd like," another voice chimed in from the hallway.

"We really need to review access to the morgue," Matias told Fred who nodded vehement agreement.

Giovanni wasn't surprised to see the young acolyte he recognizes as one of Mama Nene's followers. At this point, it seemed everyone he knew was involved in some weird way.

"Um, hi?"

"Daniel," the guy told him, holding at a hand and beaming.

Giovanni definitely remembered the smile. The guy had been friendly and unfazed all through their last encounter when they were trying to eliminate a voodoo curse.

Cookie apparently remembered him too as she quickly took his hand and carefully smoothed her curls with the other. "Hi! So, what are you doing here?" she asked.

Giovanni rolled his eyes.

"Mama Nene sent me to collect Mrs. Harris. To get her ready for the regleman. To send her home." Daniel's eyebrows knit together in caring concern as he reached for the glass carafe on the countertop, only to find himself jerked back by the hand Cookie still held.

"How do you know that's Mrs. Harris?" Cookie asked sweetly.

"You just said, *shoushou*," Daniel smiled at her and tried to wrest his hand from her grip.

"And what do you want with that cooler?" Jeremy asked, frowning at him over Cookie's shoulder.

"Really," Daniel protested. "I'm just trying to help. Mama Nene sent me."

"Really?" Matias circled around Cookie to stand near the cooler, frowning down at it.

"You study voodoo. You might even be a *houngan.* Do you know how to capture ti bon ange and contain it?" Matias asked.

"What a houngan?" Betty whispered.

"A male voodoo priest," Giovanni told her. "Mama Nene is a mambo."

"What's ti bon ange?" Betty whispered again.

Jeremy started to shush her, but Matias answered, while keeping his eyes fixed on Daniel.

"Ti bon ange is the little spirit. The body or *gros bon ange* is what animates the body, but the spirit, your personality, your likes and dislikes, your knowledge, that keeps going. It's your soul really." He sighed and leaned against the desk near the cooler, his shoulders slumping.

"And it's powerful. It's part of the divine, the cosmic breath of the universe." Matias frowned. "I can't explain it better than that, I may not even have the words right, but it's..."

"Her *ashe,*" Giovanni added, remembering what he'd been told when he'd first gone hunting for an explanation for Mrs. Harris's unusual non-death.

"Exactly!" Daniel bobbed his head emphatically. "And she was vulnerable. You didn't perform proper *dessounin.* You just left her body sitting on a porch somewhere in the mountains. I protected her. I put her in a *govi,* so she could be in the world of *Les Invisibles* for one day and one year."

"It's been three years since Mrs. Harris passed, two since she separated from her body. And we only lost her spirit last semester," Giovanni counted quietly. "You're not protecting her. You're using her."

Daniel glanced at him, then suddenly lunged for the French press on the back counter. Jeremy snatched it up and danced out of the way.

Daniel raised both hands and stepped back. His eyes darted back and forth between Jeremy and Matias. "I'm doing the task Mama Nene laid upon me," he said. "You cannot interfere in the practice of our religion –"

"You're keeping these body parts alive, aren't you?" Matias stepped in front of the cooler and as Daniel's eyes lifted, Giovanni realized that he'd been watching the cooler and carafe, not the men who held them.

"But why?" Cookie cried out. "What could you possibly want with someone's foot?"

"Practice," the tall, thin student said quietly. "We use them for practice, for research. There's a huge demand for body parts. My dad gets asked about it all the time."

The student shrugged as all eyes turned toward him. "My dad's a mortician."

"That's, that's, that's..." Cookie spluttered.

"Is that what you're doing?" Giovanni asked Daniel. "Selling body parts?" His voice came out nearly as high-pitched and squeaky as Cookie's and he didn't care.

Daniel drew himself up and look contemptuously down at all of them. "I don't owe you an explanation of my actions. You are interfering in the practice of a recognized religion."

"It's not illegal," the student said. "If someone signs a consent form. Most people don't even know the body's been broken up and resold. There's no national regulation. It's not like organ donation."

"Oh my God," Cookie waved one hand in front of her face and appeared close to tears.

Giovanni started to reach out to her in sympathy, but he was distracted by a low grinding noise. Turning, he saw Fred hunched over, propping himself up against a desk and breathing heavily. Giovanni started to say something, to reach out to him, then he realized the noise was actually Fred growling and he leaped back instinctively, pulling Cookie with him.

Fred roared, his back arching and body stretching into a fearsome height, suddenly bigger and taller even than Huntington and his shirt shredded as great hairy arms reach toward the ceiling. His thundering bellow reverberated around the room as his mouth expanded into a dark snout framing long, sharp fangs that couldn't have been more frightening if they dripped blood. Leaning forward, Fred inhaled deeply of Daniel who crumpled to his knees even as his eyes grew wide, and his hands lifted in fragile protection or perhaps supplication.

"No, wait," Daniel whispered. "I didn't do anything wrong. I didn't hurt anyone. It's not like that!"

His protests drowning in whimpers, Daniel attempted to scramble away from the great beast who loomed over him. Fred's unearthly growl lowered to a deep pitch, a vibration that hummed along bone and nerve into a frenzied panic that had Giovanni clamping his hands over his ears and cringing. Then Fred lunged forward, massive tongue darting out, and licked the side of the acolyte's face.

"It was a just a simple spell, to keep things fresh!" Daniel screamed and passed out.

A second thud followed the sound of Daniel hitting the floor and Giovanni looked around to see the thin medical student fallen in an unconscious heap as well.

Cookie gaped, open-mouthed, at both collapsed men, then swallowed hard. "What?" she whispered, "what was that?"

Giovanni looked at Jeremy who looked back and nodded. Together, they answered, "Rougarou!"

Chapter 9

"Whew! That takes a lot out of you," Fred grunted, pushing himself up from the desk he'd collapsed against. He looked himself again, a stout, elderly man except that his shirt hung in shreds around him. Matias carefully slid a chair towards him, and Fred took it gratefully, waving off any further help.

"No, no," he said. "I'm fine. We just gotta get these two out of here." And he nodded towards the men still lying on the ground.

"Don't worry," Betty said grimly. "I got body part guy covered. Daddy?" And she turned away to talk quietly into her phone.

Giovanni winced, knowing she was the daughter of the hospital president and strongly tempted to run himself, but instead he fetched Fred a glass of water. He handed one to Cookie who was sitting a little dazed as well.

Fred took the glass gratefully and drained half it off in one long gulp. He peered down at the medical student who was just sitting up, supported by Jeremy and Matias.

"Son," he said. "You gotta stop skipping meals and pulling those all-nighters."

"Yeah," Jeremy said. "And no more getting some sleep with a glass of something or other."

"You gotta maintain a healthy, balanced lifestyle," Matias told him. "You'll never get through med school otherwise."

"True," Giovanni agreed. "We'll cover for you this time, but you gotta get some sleep. What if you'd fainted on a patient?"

Skinny blinked, not really sure about what had happened, but grabbing gratefully for any lifeline. "Yeah, yeah," he agreed. "Thanks for covering for me. I'll just go get some rest." And he staggered away towards the elevator.

"Daddy's on his way." Betty turned back to the group from her phone call.

"You can't touch me," Daniel said from where he'd sat up on the floor. "I haven't broken the law."

"He's bringing the hospital lawyers," Betty continued. "He said something about theft, trespassing, breaking and entering, property damage, fraud, libel, slander, violation of union contract..." She grinned. "The lawyers thought that one up."

Daniel looked a little pale but tossed his head defiantly.

"Oh, and someone named Mama Nene is looking for you upstairs."

Daniel closed his eyes, shoulders slumping.

Giovanni thought about how vampires had chased him through the hospital and attacked Jeremy, hunting Mrs. Harris, and said, "That's not good enough. I say we let Tom and Jerry have him."

Hi roommates looked at him in mingled dismay and admiration, but Fred shook his head. "No, you got other things to do besides revenge. Go down now and get a count of what's in the basement. We gotta let Dr. Kyung know, so he can contact the families if he can."

Giovanni shuddered at the thought of informing the families about what had happened to their loved ones, but it was good motivation to begin scouring the morgue records for other mentions of Ti Bon Ange. Huntington and Matias headed down the sub-basement again to conduct a rough inventory. By the time Dr. Kyung arrived, two dark-suited gentlemen in tow, they'd carried up a dozen coolers of assorted sizes.

Giovanni was busy fitting the coolers into the back up refrigeration unit when he heard the raised voices. He didn't rush out because he was rather worried about how fresh the body parts in the cooler were going to stay now that they weren't in the same room with Mrs. Harris. He'd already locked her coffee carafe away safely in a desk drawer, whispering *it'll be okay, I'll let you out soon* as he closed the drawer. Giovanni was determined that he was not giving up Mrs. Harris's jar. He would not lose his patient a third time!

If anyone thought he was strange for talking to a jar, they didn't say. Instead, Fred barked orders, and everyone, even those who weren't technically employees, hustled boxes to and fro and didn't stop until Dr. Kyung came tearing into the morgue.

"Where is it?" he barked.

Fred's mouth twisted and he pointed to where the foot still rested in its cooler on the main desk.

"That's it?" Dr. Kyung seemed slightly taken aback. "This couldn't be just misplaced?"

Giovanni sighed and, in unconscious imitation of Fred, pointed at the backup refrigerator. Dr. Kyung stepped through the open door to see inside, then swore loudly and vehemently. Betty, who had been filing some of the wealth of papers collected in the morgue, looked askance and gently shut the file drawer she was working on.

Dr. Kyung turned at the sound of the drawer clicking closed and flushed. "Sorry, sweetie," he told his daughter, then rounded on Giovanni not nearly as sympathetic.

"What the hell have you been doing in my morgue?" he yelled.

"Don't think it's all his fault," Fred rumbled as he flipped over some of the papers still lying on the desk. "This was a pretty slick operation."

Giovanni didn't even realize he'd been slighted until Fred looked up. "It's not that you're not smart, but this took someone who knew the culture."

Fred turned to Daniel who still sat on the floor. He wasn't tied up, but Jeremy stood over him, clearly intent on preventing him from going anywhere.

"Did you reach out to just anyone or did you only tell the members of your congregation that you'd help with funeral expenses?" Fred's voice was deceptively mild, but the intent glare he aimed at Fred would have intimidated Marines.

"Yes, I'd like the answer to that question as well," Dr. Kyung added in his own version of quiet, barely restrained hostility. "You were invited into this hospital to assist patients. We made a conscious effort to reach out to the community, to all communities, so we could provide spiritual and emotional support to all faiths, not just physical care. For you to compromise that trust, is, is–"

"You bring shame to us all!" The elderly lady who hobbled in looked as fierce as any of the men confronting Daniel, but it was the sight of the people who accompanied her that upset Daniel. He cringed as he saw the crowd of acolytes all dressed in white with grim frowns file in behind Mama Nene. There were too many of them to fit in the morgue office, so they filled the hall back to the elevator, standing silent and waiting. Giovanni saw Astral among them, also grim-faced, but dressed in scrubs, not white robes.

"You know the body is sacred," Mama Nene scolded. "Whatever happens to the body affects the spirit. You told people you would care for the body, you would protect the spirit, and you lied!"

"But I did," Daniel cried out. "I took care of her. I protected her spirit."

He pointed to Giovanni, rearing to his knees. Matias and Jeremy reached for him, but a sharp gesture from Fred stopped them. They stayed poised to grab the young houngan anyway.

"He just let her wander!" Daniel protested. "I put her in a govi to care for her. I performed dessounin to separate her soul from her body."

"Her body was already gone–" Giovanni started to reply but was overridden by Mama Nene.

"You did, you did," she mocked. "You did not for the spirit. You captured ti bon ange for the power. You put her in a coffee pot! You did not honor her!"

Mama Nene's voice rose to a hoarse shout. An ugly murmur rose among her followers, words that Giovanni didn't understand, but an angry tone that was clear to all. He glanced at Astral and saw that she too was worried, eyebrows drawn together, and bottom lip caught between her teeth.

"How could you do this? How could you disrespect the ancestors, *le Bon Dieu*, like this?' Mama Nene's voice was fierce, but her shoulders slumped, and she looked every bit the frail, elderly woman she was.

Fred got up silently and offered his chair to Mama Nene. She shuddered as she sat down and Daniel cried out, real anguish in his voice, "I was trying to help! I didn't want her to become one of the Forgotten Dead."

"You lie," one of Mama Nene acolytes called out. Giovanni recognized her as the high priestess he'd met for the second time just days earlier. "Did you really think we would not honor the *Ghede lwa* too?"

"If you were really trying to help, you wouldn't have had to hire the vampires." Astral's voice was quiet, speculative, but the other people in white looked at her, surprised and baffled.

"You realized that Mrs. Harris was unburied," Astral went on. "The gros bon ang departs immediately, but her ti bon ange was not reclaimed. When she returned to hospital, you realized that she was un-reclaimed, powerful ashe. You couldn't get near her thanks to Gio's protection and the other werewolves, so you hired vampires to steal her. You wanted her because she gave you the power."

"Yeah," Jeremy added. "You used her power to preserve bodies for sale!" And he pointed towards the cooler on the desk.

"You weren't even trying to protect ti bon ange. You were using it!" The priestess cried out. "And to desecrate others?"

The murmur from the crowd grew louder and Daniel cringed on the floor at the sound.

Mama Nene raised one hand and the crowd behind her fell silent though some still shifted uneasily as they eyed one another.

"You used her to keep bodies alive. Bodies that should be dead, laid to rest, so their spirts can go to Les Invisibles," Mama Nene said.

Giovanni, watching Mama Nene, saw her close her eyes and take a deep breath. She held it for a long moment, then let it out slowly.

"You did this and for what? For money? You weren't happy in your house? You weren't happy with your car?"

Daniel opened and closed his mouth, but no words came.

Dr. Kyung stepped forward. "Ma'am, I cannot apologize enough to you or your community for this disrespect. I assure you that we will do everything in our power to return the remains of your loved ones as best we are able and will make every effort to provide final arrangements as desired."

Giovanni noticed that the lawyers cringed, but Dr. Kyung ignored them. "In addition, you should know that we are already taking steps to implement a more stable, permanent solution to morgue management with the hire of new manager."

Matias lifted one hand in a small wave, and Mama Nene nodded regally.

"Regrettably," Dr. Kyung continued, "we cannot ignore or dismiss your associate's conduct in this matter and will have to take –"

Mama Nene drew herself up as tall as her diminutive stature would allow and still looked impressive. "This man is not one of my mine," she stated, and all the people dressed in white standing in the hall turned their backs to the small group in the morgue office.

"Wait!" Daniel called out, but it was too late.

Dignity personified, Mama Nene headed to the elevator, and her acolytes, including Astral, followed, not speaking, not turning, not reacting even as Daniel called after them. When the last one stepped on the elevator, Daniel pursed into noisy sobs.

"Well, that's that," Fred said, but of course, it wasn't. Dr. Kyung had several more, sharp comments to share, and the lawyers asked pointed questions, until eventually they took Daniel by the arms and escorted him out.

Then Astral came back downstairs with detailed instructions for Giovanni from Mama Nene on something called *Wete Mo Nan Dlo*, a ceremony that they needed to perform to send Mrs. Harris's spirit on. Giovanni was a little confused at that point not only because there was a lot of information to absorb, but also because Astral started barking instructions at everyone as well. Jeremy took immediate offense, and Matias had to drag him away too.

Cookie exchanged glances with Betty, told Astral "yeah, yeah," and strolled out arm-in-arm with her friend. Huntington stuck around long enough to murmur sympathetic noises in Astral's direction, then took off after the girls. Astral took one last look at Giovanni, said, "Well, there's no point in talking to you. I'll text you," and sashayed her way up the hall to the elevator.

Giovanni turned back from watching her walk away and jumped as he met Fred's gaze. He'd forgotten the old man, who could be unearthly quiet when he wanted. Giovanni smiled weakly at the orderly.

"You okay?" Fred asked gruffly. He looked tired as he sat at the main desk.

Giovanni thought he'd never been so exhausted in his life. He'd worked back-to-back shifts in the ER, he'd wrestled snakes and children though not at the same time, thank God, and he'd chased vampires and werewolves, even an accounting clerk from Florida once, and he'd never felt as beaten down as he did right then.

"Cheer up, Gio," Fred told him. "You got her back. Now you can do this last thing for her and send Mrs. Harris on her way."

"I suppose so," Giovanni managed. Tears of stress and fatigue were welling up again. People had to stop being nice to him!

Fred clapped him on the shoulder as he pushed himself to his feet. "It's okay, Gio," he said. "Sometimes in the end, that's all you can do for your patient."

Chapter 10

"**I**s that what you're wearing?"

Giovanni looked down at the tie Cookie fussed with. She rolled her eyes and stepped back.

"He looks fine," she told Jeremy who lounged in the door to Giovanni's room.

"He looks like an undertaker," Jeremy laughed and pushed himself off the doorjamb.

"Nice!" Cookie replied, and she slapped at him as she pushed past Jeremy.

Jeremy snorted and turned to follow her. "Seriously," he told Giovanni as he went, "you look fine."

Giovanni frowned at his reflection, then sighed and turned to follow his roommates. He'd gotten the suit when he graduated college, and it was probably still stylish enough, but it felt awkward and uncomfortable. Three years of working in scrubs may have toned his body, but considerably relaxed his tolerance for formal dress.

He'd wanted to look good, however, for Mrs. Harris's final send off. Jeremy had gone all out, dressing in a dark tux with tails and snowy white shirt. Matias told him no to a top hat and sunglasses and Jeremy has argued until Fred stopped them with an abrupt, "No! That's not the lwa we need."

So, Jeremy had compromised with pale gold brocade vest, and Matias wore a matching tie with a grey vest under his charcoal suit. Cookie naturally wore something sparkly, short and sleeveless in pink. Jeremy made noises about dressing for a night club, but under his breath where everybody could ignore him. Giovanni thought she looked wonderful and frowned at his reflection again in the old mirror that topped a hall table as he came down the stairs. Then he squeaked and jumped back hurriedly as the front door flew open.

"Sorry," Anthony barked, not sounding sorry. He was dressed in uniform, crisp and belligerent down to his polished shoes and up to his close-cropped hair.

"He really is," a soft voice added, and Dr. Smith followed her husband into the house. She frowned at the former sergeant, but only in a mild way. She was dressed in a dark suit with a snug skirt she tugged at automatically.

"You look nice." She smiled at Giovanni.

He laughed and shrugged. "Not scrubs though."

"Tell me about it," Dr. Smith responded. "I'm still fighting baby weight," and she tugged at her skirt again.

"You look great," Giovanni told her in all sincerity.

"Hey!" Anthony and Cookie chimed in together and then looked at each other, startled.

"Listen," Giovanni started nervously. He wasn't sure what to say to Anthony exactly, how to explain what he was going to do, what he had to do for the man's aunt. She had been his last living relative after all.

"It's okay." Anthony clapped Giovanni on the shoulder. "It's better this way."

Dr. Smith touched the sergeant lightly on the arm and he reached out to take her hand. "And she got to see the baby and all, so..."

Anthony swallowed hard, then snapped, "Alright! Let's move out."

Giovanni followed the couple into the living room where Fred was supervising final preparations. He greeted the sergeant with a firm hand clasp and one arm thrown wide in invitation. Cookie bustled about, fussing with the arrangement of plates and platters of food on every surface while Jeremy fussed at her.

"Look at all this food," Giovanni whispered to Matias who peeping out of the kitchen. "How many people are coming?"

"We're supposed to stay up all night," Matias whispered back. "We haven't done all the rituals in the right order, so we're including all that we can. Help me with the coffee."

Giovanni looked around Matias at the commercial coffee urn sitting on the kitchen counter. "Where did you get that? No, no, that will never do!"

"I got it from work," Matias started, but Giovanni ignored him.

"Break out the Delonghi," he said.

The two men had all of the house's various coffee makers percolating, and Jeremy was just starting to protest when Mama Nene and her congregation showed up. Astral noted the row of coffee makers and smirked as she passed by, helping Mama Nene to a seat on the screened porch. The high priestess rolled her eyes as she passed but didn't say anything either. The rest of the congregation bustled about filling plates and cups. Giovanni was baffled, remembering Mama Nene's admonishment against caffeine until Jeremy leaned over and whispered, "They have to be ready for horse. Everyone else just has to stay awake."

The congregation certainly seemed prepared to do that. They brought in food and drink and ate and drank. A group of men and one girl set up a ring of drums in a semi-circle in the backyard near the barbeque and begin playing. Just about the time Giovanni thought Mrs. Harris's sendoff was going to dissolve into a party, the congregation gathered outside and started chanting. The music was cheerful, not the solemn masses he'd attended with his nonnas growing up, but he knew enough about voodoo to know the women whirling around in white skirts in his backyard believed just as firmly as his nonnas did.

Swallowing hard, he pulled Mrs. Harris's glass carafe out of the kitchen cabinet where he'd hidden it. Setting it down on the kitchen counter, he stopped to straighten his tie and tuck his shirt in again.

"It's time," Jeremy said from the door to the living area. He swallowed hard as well, then made a come-on gesture with one hand.

Giovanni nodded and picked up the carafe that contained Mrs. Harris. He took a deep breath, then felt tears pricking as he turned to the back door.

"It's okay, dude. It's okay." Jeremy placed one hand on his shoulder. Matias took his place on his other side, looking grim. Anthony also looked grim, but then Anthony always looked grim.

By the time the quartet stepped outside, Giovanni was crying freely, hard enough that he needed his friends' hands to guide him. He didn't even try to wipe away the tears though because he didn't want to take a chance on spilling Mrs. Harris. He wasn't embarrassed because he wasn't alone. Cookie stood next to Betty, her face twisted in miserable sympathy, the ghostly figure of a gangster moll sobbing behind her.

Still chanting, the high priestess danced in a widening circle to where the grass was worn away just beyond the barbecue. Someone has laid out rows of candles, and the high priestess dipped and swayed as she lit them. Then she turned to bow to Fred to stood just off to one side. "Papa Legba, open the gate," she called to the crowd. "*C'est le geste qui prime.*"

Fred moved to the bare spot next to the barbecue. He was dressed in a grey suit, noticeably frayed, and leaned on a heavy stick. Under his feet, etched in the ground, was a complicated cross, drawn in the dirt with chalk and lots of extra curlicues. As Giovanni's small procession arrived, the chanting crowd fell silent.

"We're here today to release Mrs. Harris's spirit to the forest to dwell in trees and grottos, to wait to be reborn," Fred began. He raised the hand holding his staff and continued, "Mrs. Harris lived a long life and a good one. After she's lived sixteen lives, may her spirit go on to Damballah Wedo and become part of the Djo, the cosmic breath that envelops the universe. May we all be able to live and grow the same." And Fred bowed as he stepped to one side, swinging his staff in open invitation towards the grassy field rimmed with Georgia pines behind the house.

Mama Nene leaned forward in the lawn chair she occupied next to the barbecue. "Send her home, son," she said, her voice as deep and growling as Fred's.

Giovanni nodded and gently put the coffee press on the ground. Holding it steadily with one hand, he unscrewed the top and set it aside. "Mrs. H?" he managed.

"Shoushou?" The faint whisper could be heard in the silence. The only visible change was a faint dimming of the silvery liquid in the glass jar, but Giovanni knew that voice.

Giovanni closed his eyes in relief. "Yeah, it's me," he said. "Come on out, Mrs. H."

"Oh shoushou," the faint quavering voice continued. "I was so cold, and I couldn't find Jeremy. I need to find Jeremy."

"It's okay, Mrs. H.," and Giovanni knew it was even if he couldn't see Mrs. Harris. "I've got Jeremy. He's safe."

"It's time to go, Mrs. H. Can you see the trees? You can go there and wait till you have another life. You'll be safe there."

"Trees?" The faint whisper sounded doubtful. "Anthony's in the trees? I need to find Anthony."

"He's okay," Dr. Smith whispered hoarsely, fighting back tears. "It's okay, *Tante*. I've got him," and she clasped Anthony's hand. Anthony nodded and made a circling motion with the other, too choked up to speak.

"Everyone's safe, Mrs. H. You did it." Giovanni said, and his voice grew stronger. "You can go home now. It's time to go home."

Perhaps it was his imagination, but he thought he saw a faint impression drift towards the open expanse of lawn. "Do you see the trees, Mrs. H?" he added.

"Oh, shoushou, it's so pretty!" the whisper came, and Giovanni felt as much as saw Mrs. Harris move away over the lawn to the line of trees where the Civil War ghosts drifted apart, then turned, to follow her.

The high priestess called out something Giovanni didn't hear, and the drumming started up again. Giovanni hastily snatched the coffee press out of the way of the spinning congregation and realized it had gone completely dark, only ordinary water sloshing in it now.

"Wait, wait," called the sobbing moll next to Cookie. "I want to go too. I want a swell wingding, not these dewdropper palookas!" and Giovanni saw her racing by, a breeze picking up in her wake.

"Me too," another flapper called out and the breeze around the barbecue grew, tossing cups and napkins along with skirts and robes. The acolytes chanted louder and stomped harder, raising even more dust.

"What are you trying to pull here?" A voice roared. "I ain't doing the big sleep for some dame! Give her the gate, boys!" And the breeze grew into a whirlwind that buffeted people with paper plates and leaves as a stream of grey figures in suits ran for the road in front of the house.

Giovanni stood gaping after them until a harsh laugh broke the silence. "Ha, ha, ha," Mama Nene chortled. "Got rid of them ghosts after all. Ha, ha, ha."

"Fabulous," Cookie commented as she came up beside Giovanni, sarcasm unmistakable.

"Um, you did want to get rid of them," Giovanni started.

Cookie reached up and cupped his cheek briefly. "Not as much as they wanted to ditch their piker boyfriends. You okay?"

"Yeah," Giovanni managed. He reached up and took Cookie's hand. "I got something for you," he blurted out. "It's not too sparkly. I can't afford a really big diamond. It's more of a promise ring if you'd like."

Cookie stared at him, eyes opened wide.

"I just thought you might come with me wherever I get a match. I'm pretty sure I'm done at this hospital," Giovanni added. He was nervous about how she might react, but he was determined to ask anyway. Being seen as crazy didn't worry him as much as it used to.

Cookie nodded, her mouth twisting, then she jumped and hugged Giovanni all at the same time, so his head bobbed up and down in her grasp.

"Oh, yes, yes, yes," Cookie cried. "I will totally go with you!"

"Well, that's less of the *vévé* we need to erase," the high priestess murmured as she watched the happy couple scuff up the carefully chalked cross in the dirt, "however –" and she waved at the musicians who broke into an upbeat rhythm once more as acolytes swirled in joyful abandon across the yard.

Matias, watching Giovanni and Cookie wander off lost in each other, grinned ruefully. "We're gonna have to find another roommate."

"She has got it bad," Jeremy added as Matias pulled him into his arms and into the sweep of the dance. "She didn't even stop to change her shoes."

"He's staying right here," Fred told them as he danced by, the high priestess circling with him. "The hospital's sending him to the CDC for his residency. Infectious Diseases, maybe epidemiology."

Anthony whirled by, looking almost as curious as his wife. "The CDC?" he asked.

Fred shrugged. "Gotta be prepared," he said. "What if there's a real outbreak?"

Now it's the end!

Don't miss out!

Visit the website below and you can sign up to receive emails whenever Kathy Bryson publishes a new book. There's no charge and no obligation.

https://books2read.com/r/B-A-VMSC-KYBQB

BOOKS 2 READ

Connecting independent readers to independent writers.

Also by Kathy Bryson

The Fayetteville Fairies
Feeling Lucky
Restless Spirits
Fighting Mad

The Med School Series
Giovanni In Med School
Giovanni Goes To Med School
Giovanni Meets A Coven
Giovanni Joins The Werewolves
Giovanni Dines With Vampires
Giovanni Haunts The Hospital
Giovanni Rests In Pieces

Standalone
Kneehigh2AGrasshopper

Watch for more at https://kathybrysonbooks.com.